SABRE BLUE SOCIETY
(SABSO)

Featuring Homicide Detective Johnny Vero

fred berri

SABRE BLUE SOCIETY
(SABSO)

Featuring Homicide Detective Johnny Vero

****

****

Reader Awareness

The story herein is for a mature audience containing adult material that includes coarse language, sexual content, and violence.

Award-winning 5 Star Author of
Cousins' Bad Blood
Ten Cents a Dance
Bullets Before Dawn-Murder in Chinatown
Murder on Contadora Island
Adventures of Carmelo
(a continuing series of children's learning stories)

Reader's Favorite provides professional reviews for authors and has earned the respect of renowned publishers such as Random House, Simon & Schuster and Harper Collins. Reader's Favorite has received the Best Websites for Authors and Honoring Excellence awards from the Association of Independent Authors. Reader's Favorite also tries to help those in need by donating books and income each year to St. Jude Children's Research Hospital.

"Twist, turn and bend the truth.
Now it's fiction." © fred berri

****
fredberri.com

"Sometimes it's the very people who no one imagines anything of, who do the things no one can imagine."

The Imitation Game - Christopher Morcom

Dedication

My Lola, who has always been there.

To the Blue Brotherhood.

****

NOTE FROM THE AUTHOR

This story is fictional. Any names, characters, places, or situations are purely coincidental and are a "fougasse"[1] Any similarity to real persons, living or dead is coincidental and not intended by the author, except historical events, historical dates, or any actual locations, and facts.

---

[1] Fougasse /fuːˈɡaːs/ is a term used for "fake" or not real. The word originated back in the seventeenth century to describe a fake rock that was filled with explosives during wars. Soldiers would step on these fake rocks, exploding the bomb and causing serious injury or death. So, the rock being fake or not real was termed a *fougasse*. This novel is a fougasse.

SABRE BLUE SOCIETY (SABSO)[2]

Featuring Homicide Detective Johnny Vero
Series #3

---

[2] *Sabre Blue Society (SABSO)* is a fictious unit of the NYPD (New York Police Department) created by author, fred berri.

Prologue

New York City's District Attorney, Molly Penett, Detective Johnny Vero's lover and long-time associate, sat nervously in the audience. She knows what Johnny and his partner, Billy Bradshaw, will face. Molly knows firsthand that danger and the unexpected comes with being part of this elite group, the Sabre Blue Society. Her father, now deceased, was a onetime member of this shining unit.

She was reminded of the Daily Globe headline when he was with the South-Central Police Precinct and the perils it produced…

"COP SHOT IN CHINATOWN BACK ON THE JOB:
IS OUR CITY SAFE?"

A New Day-A New Dawn-A New Year

Chapter 1

Lieutenant Johnny Vero gave periodic whimsical thoughts on being here, at the ready, for induction into the Sabre Blue Society—*SABSO*.

SABSO, a specialized elite unit, is part of the NYPD, dealing far beyond the depths of the department's undercover and Internal Affairs brothers in blue. The mission of the Sabre Blue Society is to engage and address high-priority issues such as international organized crime, arms control intelligence, and a broad range of criminal activities. Their jurisdiction reaches outside the boundaries of the five boroughs of New York. John Q Public recognizes it as more of an international organization with a close working relationship with Interpol.

This ceremony differs greatly from other NYPD promotional ceremonies. They limit it to a few dignitaries and immediate family members to uphold its integrity and maintain inner secrecy. The public knows it as the NYPD Task Force.

In attendance with Molly is the Chief of Police, the Police Commissioner, the Mayor, Johnny's daughter Angie, and Cardinal Fermi, for the benediction. Molly accepts that many need the strength of prayer, although its promise seems unclear.

Johnny Vero, the most decorated Detective in New York City, and his partner through the years, Billy Bradshaw, are both inductees.

The Sabres offered, Molly, Angie, and Nancy, Detective Bradshaw's wife, rise with pride, applause bringing smiles and tears of joy. Their eyeliner runs like downhill skiers in a race. Each notices the other and laughs at the silliness it portrays.

Chapter 2

Johnny and Molly hadn't decided which way to go. Should Johnny keep his bachelor apartment he'd lived in since his divorce many years ago? His ex-wife Simone now lives in Europe. Or should he and Molly cohabit at her place near the United Nations building? It's a personal decision; Angie has been on her own for some time.

Some days they calmly discussed living together; other days they heated up into a full-blown war that resulted in the exciting makeup sex they both loved. Molly often wondered if Johnny instigated those battles knowing what lie ahead.

"Johnny, my gut tells me you're on dangerous waters going after Griff and Carol Lynne, even though you have SABSO behind you. I've been involved with some of their cases as the D.A. These assignments are dangerous, taking you wherever and whenever, and I'm okay with it because that's what you want. Last year chasing those criminals almost got you killed, although your partially shot off ear is kind of sexy. I know you want to go after the two perps that got away with those murders in Chinatown. So do I. I want to prosecute those bastards!"

"You're right, Molly. Griff, our smuggler, is lurking, working his prostitutes and selling shipments of opium somewhere in this world, maybe with that psychopath, Carol Lynne, he had as a connection. I say he's coming back here. You can't teach an old dog new tricks. He knows where to get the bone," Johnny answered.

"Even though both Ralph "the Trucker" Mariozo, and his cousin, Jimmy "the Rat" Enrizzi, are resting in Woodlawn Cemetery, their hands reach out of the grave. The mob still has a contract out on you and Billy. Griff and Carol Lynne are an extension of Ralph and Jimmy's organization," Molly reminded him.

"Thanks for your concern, Molly; you're so right. I love you," Johnny murmured, kissing her neck before handing Molly her wine. "You're a wonderful woman. I'm glad we're together." He sipped his Old Crow bourbon whiskey.

We're not getting any younger. I want that ring, Molly thought.

Let's put on Coleman Hawkins, your jazz favorite, and see where the night takes us, shall we?" A large grin accompanied Johnny's suggestion.

*"The Past is never where you think
you left it."*

Katherine Anne Porter

Chapter 3

The Sabre Blue Society and the Federal Bureau of Investigation have their headquarters at One Federal Plaza, known throughout law enforcement as the Feed House because NYC's top cases were fed to the FBI and SABSO there.

Detectives Johnny Vero and Bradshaw entered the Feed House lobby as usual. An old-time friend and confidential informant, Willy, stood at his shoeshine stand as usual. He gave Johnny his signal, letting him know he has something important to tell him.

"Ah, Detectives, I ain't seen you two peas in a pod, long time comin'," Willy said in his combined Mobile, Alabama, and Spokane, Washington, accent. "Let's see those Florsheims up here, Lieutenant," tapping Johnny's shoe with direction. "How 'bout you, Detective. C'mon now. Willy sees those hoofers be needin' some lovin'. Put yours right up on this side, Detective. Ol' man Willy ain't gunna bite you, ya know."

"Willy, what do you have for me?" Johnny asks, looking down at Willy who is giving Johnny's shoes a once over before starting his routine.

"Lieutenant, ya know I got some goods for you. This gunna make your hair stand up on the back of your neck, ya know. It's bin a long time, since that colored guy and the Chinaman came sittin' right where you are. This time it be the colored guy alone. Ya all remember. The one with the big scar 'cross his face. Man, that cat sure is ugly, uh huh, like somebody whoop him with that ugly stick. Now let me tells you 'bout ugly. My wife's—"

"Willy," Johnny snapped, "another day about your mother-in-law. We don't have all day."

"I see what you mean, Lieutenant. Alright. He don't talk much, like your partner here, ya know. So, I try to talk, ya know, to all my customers. Some like it and some don't. He's a don't. So, I keep my mouth shut until he says, "Mr. Willy, do a lot of cops, maybe detectives, come for a shine?"

"Jesus, Billy, look around. That son-of-a-bitch Griff might be right here looking at us. Maybe he's got the contract out on us," Johnny said.

"Nah!" Billy answered nonchalantly. "He wouldn't be that stupid, would he"?

"Maybe not him, but some other perp could be sizing us up to see what we do and where we go for a set-up hit," Johnny said with trepidation. "Willy, anything else?"

"No, sir. Just lettin' you know that he be right here. He looks like the trouble you've been lookin' for, Lieutenant." Willy finished with his 'rag popping,' humming to the beat of a bit of jazz. He could make shoes shine like you were looking in a mirror.

"Billy, do you believe the balls on this guy walking right into the Feed House? Griff knows he's wanted by us along with that psycho Carol Lynne. I'll tell Molly and pass it along to them who need to know. This was good, Willy, real good," handing Willy a saw buck for the two shines.

"Lieutenant, ten bucks," Willy howled. "God bless you, Lieutenant! 1950 gunna be a good year for shur."

Chapter 4

The Teletype at the SABSO office spits out paper all day—information and requests for help with cases other law enforcement agencies can't put to rest. Johnny and Billy rummage through their assignments in the pages torn from the teleprinter and dropped off to the office they share.

"Johnny, you need to see this," Billy said, "but be discreet about it. This is in tune to what Willy just told us," handing him the information.

"Mother Mary of God!" Johnny yelped, flashing back to his father's favorite oath, amongst others, particularly after a few whiskies. Johnny could still recall the day his father was killed on the job. A beat cop, he walked the streets on the lower East Side of Manhattan in a tough neighborhood known as 'Hell's Kitchen.' Davy Crockett created its name in 1835 when he said, 'In my part of the country, when you meet an Irishman, you find a first-rate gentleman; but these are worse than savages; they are too mean to swab hell's kitchen,' putting the residents of that area in a class lower than savages. Officer Vero died there, in the infamous *Hell's Kitchen*.

"Johnny, you okay?" Billy's concern jolted him back.

"Yeah. I just got a flashback."

"Your old man?" Billy asked.

"It never goes away, Billy. Something like Nancy's first husband, Roger, committing suicide.

"It's not right how life gets in the way when we try to make plans," directing his partner back to the Teletype he held.

"Hmm. I'll think on that. This page printed day before yesterday, according to the date. Jesus, we need to get more help around here."

"Tell that to the judge," Billy said, using an old adage.

Johnny stared at the printed page.

> I know what you're looking for. I have it. I told you months ago when you could not find me. It's my insurance policy.
>
> CL

"CL, that bitch! That's Carol Lynne for sure. I still can't figure out how that murdering psycho got away. She's on everyone's top most wanted list, even Interpol's. We got to get her, Billy."

"And Griff. We know he's here from what Willy told us. How coincidental is it, hearing from both of them? Why did that pair suddenly pop up? How the fuck did they slip through our fingers to begin with? Could be they're working together, jawboning us. Is there a way to find out where the Teletype originated?" Billy commented.

"Nah! Tele, from the Greek, means far off, but we have an idea where she is," Johnny said.

"Oh yeah, the Navy trained you in Cryptography."

"Remember the last message she sent? She has Monica's journal with all the john's names and their information from the whorehouse and bar Monica ran at the Budapest Hotel."

"How can I forget the Nostalgia Café and the times we frequented that joint? The only way she got that journal was by murdering Monica. She told us in her message last year she got it from Monica's room in France. And you know whose names besides all the City's dignitaries are in that journal, don't you?" Billy asked rhetorically, not expecting his partner to answer.

"Some things we don't forget. Who knew Monica kept records in a journal? We got to get that fucking book." Johnny's words were more than a mere suggestion. "That journal could ruin a lot of lives. Carol Lynne is holding a great insurance policy that could buy her freedom from all those murders she committed."

"If she were in front of me, Johnny, I'd change the term *Beat Cop* from our flat-foot rookie days into a verb."

Johnny sighed, then cracked a smirk. "I catch your drift, but then you'd wind up in the hoosegow. I need you here, big daddy. At least we've got her fiancé and accomplice, Dr. Dean Paul from the medical examiner's office, tucked away in his cell."

"It's hard to believe that so much time has gone by since the atrocities and Chinatown murders she took part in," Billy pitched in. "Hmm. Maybe it's time to pay the doctor a visit. Whatt ya think?"

Johnny nodded

"I'll call the prison, let them know we're coming."

Chapter 5

The heavy rain made the windshield wipers work hard. They created a melodic swishing sound that could easily lull Johnny to sleep. Billy had turned the police radio scanner off. Johnny rode shotgun. Passing through Chinatown, the ride to the West Side Highway stirred up old memories of Billy, Molly, and him solving the eleven murders that stemmed from there. Although it was over a year, the details of every one were clear—who, what, and where they all took place, the fire in the prison, the suicide of his most notorious collar, Alvise LaPoshio—indelibly cataloged in his memory. All that was in the recent past, and Griff and Carol Lynne's disappearance was like a plague, eating at him. The ride to Sing Sing Prison in Ossining seemed to take forever. Even for the pair of hard-boiled cops, Route 9A along the Palisades of the Hudson River was breathtaking, whatever the season.

"Nothing is so well learned as that which is discovered."

Socrates

Chapter 6

After a thorough inspection of the NYC Detective's credentials, the guard in the gatehouse sent instructions to the tower guard to open the drive-through gate. He directed them to a specific spot where they parked their unmarked NYPD-issue sedan. Dwarfed by the ten-foot steel door, another guard armed with a Thompson submachine gun, also known as the "Tommy Gun," secured the prison entrance. A sign overhead read, "ENTER HERE."

"Howdy, Detectives. You know the routine by now. Check in down the hall," said the guard, giving the signal to release the lock.

Johnny and Billy entered as directed. It had been a long time since their last visit for prisoner interrogations, but the traditional way always stood its ground.

"Sign in here Detectives and surrender your firearms. We'll give 'em back to you when you leave. Surrender any back-ups too," said the officer in the cage. A long time had passed since either of them carried back-up weapons strapped to their ankles.

Hmm, food for thought. Johnny glanced at his partner.

"We're good, Sergeant," Billy responded, eager to get on with it. He placed his weapon on the counter alongside Johnny's.

"Both of you sign with your shield numbers and let's see your mugs on some picture identification," the guard behind the barred cage said, his manner matter of fact. He checked their signatures and profile against their I.D.s. "Okay. You're all set. We have some new *go throughs* since our last disturbance, Detectives," he said, buzzing them into a two-step process of barred doors. "Just follow the arrows on the wall. It'll get you where you want to go."

"Thanks, Sergeant, we'll catch you on the rebound," Johnny politely answered.

"Jesus, Johnny, this is a completely new maze. I don't remember hearing about any disturbances here, have you?" Billy asked as they picked up their pace.

"No. Wow! They've added, what? I've counted three more locked pass throughs with the cameras following us so the doors unlock from a remote station."

"Ah, I hope this is the last gate," Billy said.

"Right this way, Detectives. Your prisoner is in this room." Three armed guards stood in a cluster. "We'll be right outside the door," one of them said.

"Holy shit! It's you two," Dr. Dean Paul said, one hand cuffed to the iron clasp in the middle of the table. "Either of you flatfoots got a smoke? I hoped, just maybe, I was getting a hooker for my exemplary behavior."

Billy took out a cigarette, handed it over, then lit it.

"So, flatfoots, or should I say dicks? What the fuck brings you here?" Paul took a long drag, a habit too few and far between indulgences. *Anything in this hellhole I can get some pleasure from.*

"We heard from your fiancé, Carol Lynne," Billy said, staring at Paul's eyes to read his reaction.

"Who?" Paul asked.

Both Johnny and Billy sneered. "Cut the bullshit. You know you jerk off thinking about her," Billy taunted. "Is she still your fiancé?

"Hmm, maybe," Paul replied, exhaling cigarette smoke across the table at them. He betrayed nothing with his cavalier manner. "So, what do you want from me? You must want something. You didn't take an hour-and-half ride for the scenery. Besides, it's over a year that you and that f—"

"Don't be nasty," Johnny cut him off, knowing where he was going with his sarcasm.

"You, Detective, and that... beautiful young D.A. were here. She held my hand and promised me she would put in the paperwork to get me moved. Yet, I'm still here in this fucking rat hole," Paul said.

"You're right, Dr. Paul," Johnny said, trying not to bruise his ego any further. He knew the State stripped his medical license from him. Johnny wanted information. If he had the power, he'd provide him with a hooker to get it. Since he couldn't, he had to use other tactics. "Would you like some coffee?"

"Maybe a shot of bourbon," Paul snickered. "So..." he spread his hands, waiting for a response to his quandary.

"C'mon Doc," a reluctant Billy used his former title, giving him a little credence. "We told you we heard from her. Don't give us the brush off. We figure you can give us more than bupkis." He added, wiggling his eyebrows in appreciation. "She sure is a looker. We found photos of you and her in the Yonkers house. Would you like them? I can arrange that."

"I don't like you looking at them," Dr. Paul said. *You scumbag!*

"We've checked with the warden about your mail. You're not off the hook here. Show us her letters. No rhubarb, give it to us straight," Billy said emphatically, calling his bluff since they hadn't checked.

"Tell me, Detective. If I give you what you want, intel on her where-a-bouts, what's in it for me? You know, quid pro quo, this for that. You dicks use it all the time. What kind of deal can you offer me? How about getting me out of here like your dame promised?"

"Listen, we can't commute your sentence, but maybe we can get you into a better situation in another facility closer to family. How 'bout your own cell, a radio, and books? I can get you out of the laundry, maybe work in the prison library? I might could wrangle a position teaching inmates in a classroom setting. It would be nice and cushy. That I can promise you. The D.A. started your paperwork way back. You worked for the City. You know how the bullshit red-tape works. How does that sound, Doctor?" Johnny said, giving a performance.

"Guard, take me to my cell, so I can get these dicks what they want."

Chapter 7

Johnny began reading the SABSO research report handed him. "The postmarks on the envelopes Carol Lynne sent to Dr. Dean Paul in prison show they originated from 'Valle d'Aosta, Italy.' Further, the report gave the coordinates as 45.7389 degrees N, 7.4262 degrees E.

"That don't tell me if a bear shits in the woods or if a tree makes a sound when it falls in the forest," Billy clamored.

"Listen. You must remember something from your Navy days," Johnny said, beginning the report.

The Aosta Valley. A mountainous region in northwestern, Italy, bordered by Auvergne-Rhone-Alpes, France to the west; Valais, Switzerland, to the north; and Piedmont, Italy, to the south and east. Italian and French are the official languages."

"What the hell good is that information going to do for us, Johnny?" Billy asked in frustration.

"A lot, Billy. Look; here's a map. This gives us a visual of how close this place is to France and Switzerland. Now that we have SABSO behind us. . ." Johnny raised his eyebrows and shrugged his shoulders like it was no big deal to get on a plane and go to Europe. He watched as Billy grasped the possibility. "What do you think?"

"Oh no, Johnny. Another trek around a foreign country like we had to do a few years back when we went after the maniacal French serial killer, Jean-Paul Vincent? Another round of Interpol and working with that French Inspector Laurent? I won't be able to live with Nancy if I take another trip to Europe without her."

"As they say, *c'est la vie*. When we retire, you can travel anywhere you want. Your old lady is loaded. That inheritance from Roger's parents, that clothing factory, set her up. They were good to her after their son committed suicide," Johnny recalled.

"Yeah, they were there for her. They loved Nancy. When Roger's unit pushed forward to stop the Japanese from taking the Aleutian Islands during the war, he got his legs blown off. The U.S. lost that battle. His parents knew he wasn't right after that. Roger lost a helluva lot more than Nancy. She lost her husband, but he lost his will to live. He was a hero. Sad, very sad," Billy chimed in, remorseful, remembering a significant moment of time.

"You know one of my favorite sayings, Billy. Life gets in the way when we're making plans."

"Ahem," Billy cleared his throat. "Yeah, it seems that way. What else do we have?" trying to move past his memories.

"Well, to start, we have to put in all the bullshit request forms to get the ball rolling. SABSO makes it a lot easier than

South Central ever did. I have to tell Molly, and I'm sure it won't be easy for you to tell Nancy. Why don't we all go to *Delmonico's Steak House*? We can tell them over a prime rib and drinks. Maybe go to the *No It Awl Jazz Club* for a late show after. We'll show 'em a good time. They'll love it," Johnny suggested.

"Yeah, but my wallet won't," murmured Billy.

"Too bad Leelee Gaye won't be performing. She was an incredible entertainer."

"Hmm, Leelee Gaye. Who woulda figured she was undercover FBI?"

Chapter 8

Life never seemed maudlin to Johnny, even when he drank. *I need a vacation. I should go see Oma, in Florida,* remembering his daughter Angie's name for his mom. She would be happy to see them all again. *Maybe after me and Billy get back from Europe.*

Stretched out on the couch suited him just fine. He never liked the cop bars and the retelling of stories: shoot outs; who killed who; who got fucked with Internal Affairs; and who retired to Arizona or Florida. Sitting quietly, sipping his Old Crow whiskey, memories of his studies at the Manhattan School of Music and playing his cello absorbed him. His mind quiescent, the classical music he loved relaxed him, until it was all interrupted.

"Johnny, I'm back," Molly called out. "Where are you? I have a surprise."

"I'm on the couch, Molly. What's the surprise?" he asked.

"If I told you, it wouldn't be a surprise. I'll be two minutes," she called out. "Okay, I'm ready. C'mon in here. When you reach the door, keep your eyes closed. Don't open them until I tell you."

Johnny followed her instructions implicitly, looking forward to Molly's girly surprise. *Maybe a new red dress for our night out to Delmonico's and the Jazz Club. She loves to be the cat's meow.*

"Knock, knock, I'm here."

"Open your eyes and open the door like you were walking into a fresh crime scene."

Johnny's eyes widened like a kid in a candy store. Molly reclined against the propped pillows of the bed, exquisite in a lace see-through negligee, white as the driven snow. *Way better than a new dress!*

"Very nice," he said, looking forward to peeling it off her.

Chapter 9

Detectives Vero and Bradshaw took the stairs to Molly's office one floor below to brief her on the Griff and Carol Lynne investigation, the two that got away from Chinatown.

"She's in," Louise jerked her head toward the office door while she answered a telephone. Molly's secretary buzzed her as the Detectives passed her desk.

Molly's office reflected a woman's taste, government-issue with feminine touches, a contrast to Johnny and Billy's stark office. She conducted casual meetings in the sitting area at the far end of the room. The comfortable, rich dark brown leather couch and chairs harmonized perfectly with her decor, just as Molly herself looked chic yet professional as she met the demands of her position every day.

Hanging directly behind her desk at eye level was an American Flag under glass, framed and folded in the ceremonial triangle. This flag had draped her father's casket at his funeral.

"I can't believe those two are still at large. What is it, a year, fourteen months, and those bastards are still out there doing who knows what and to whom?" Molly asked.

"We know, Molly. Don't think it hasn't had an effect on Johnny and me. It doesn't go away," Billy answered with concern. "Show her, Johnny."

"Show me? Show me what, Detective?" Molly asked, looking at Billy.

"This," Johnny said, handing Molly the envelopes Dr. Paul had retrieved from his cell.

"Scented love letters?" she scoffed. "You know as well as I do what he does after reading them and sniffing her perfume. So what? What does he expect for these?" Molly questioned, stirring concern in the Detectives.

"He certainly remembers you, Molly. He's stewing in his own pot about you not getting him outta there over a year ago." Billy's comment ignited Molly's Italian temperament.

"That little—"

"Here, Molly, this too," Johnny cut her off, handing Molly the SABSO report on the whereabouts of Carol Lynne. "We got this off the wire. Before you read that, I told Dr. Paul this time we'd get him transferred out of the laundry into the library, or maybe to another facility, teaching inmates."

"Teaching? Teaching what? How to slice and dice people? That little fuck!"

Giving the Teletype a thorough read, Molly reached the portion that she re-read aloud:

I know what you're looking for. I have it. I told you months ago when you could not find me. It's my insurance policy. CL.

"What the fuck is she talking about? Do either of you know?" she asked, slamming her hand down on the desk. If smoke could come out of Molly's ears, you would have needed an extinguisher to put out the fire. "What is this insurance policy and when the fuck did she tell you about this?" Molly demanded with suspicion and anger. "It says months ago. Jesus Christ! I never saw or heard this before. Speak up, Detectives," addressing them by their titles, not as her lover or as a friend. Molly questioned them, her raised voice harsh, just short of screaming.

"Miss. Penett," her secretary's voice sounded across Molly's intercom. "Everyone here is looking toward your door. I thought you ought to know."

"Molly, simmer down," Johnny added, his hands motioning palms down in front of him. "Please listen to what Louise just said," Johnny encouraged her.

Molly realized the depth of her anger was unjustified, but she wasn't letting them off the hook.

"Johnny's right. Ease up, Molly. Johnny and I were hashing this out this morning. We're not sure what Carol Lynne's talking about when she mentions an insurance policy. We know nothing with regard to a bargaining chip she thinks she has." Billy jumped to their defense, although they knew Carol referred to Monica's journal in her coffer. They hadn't informed Molly of the journal's existence. What Carol hadn't told the Detectives is what she wanted in return.

"Well, Gentlemen, it seems that our run-a-way is tired of being on the lam, which makes no sense to me. Maybe she's looking for some sort of deal. So, what we need to find out is what this proverbial ace in the hole is that she's blabbing about and what she wants for it," Molly stated. "Look, I know that you are with SABSO and they have their own way of doing things. It's just—"

"We understand, Molly," Johnny appeased. "We brought this to you, knowing we're all together in that debacle. Going forward, you're the one who will have to prosecute her, if we ever get her back in the States."

"That fucking lunatic will get a deal alright. Deal! When fucking pigs fly," she said, pointing to the air. Leave it to me. As far as our jail bird, we can make that happen if he continues to cooperate," Molly said, not yet down from her feverish tantrum. "Now, get out of my office, the both of you."

****

"Jesus, that went well," Billy stated as the elevator doors closed, taking them to the floor below. His tongue-in-cheek wasn't a stretch. "I've never seen Molly like that."

"We all got two sides, don't we, Billy? Some have three or four. Look at Griff, Carol Lynne, and Dr. Paul for Christ's sake. Maybe they have half a dozen sides. Crazy psychopaths," Johnny answered. "We know Molly's upset. We'll smooth her feathers. Our foursome to *Delmonico's* and *The No It Awl Jazz Club* will stroke some of those feathers. She enjoys the glitter and glamor. I bet Nancy does too."

"Sure as shit, Johnny," Billy quipped. "Where do we go from here?"

"South-Central and see Captain Sullivan."

Deja Vu

Chapter 10

Hearing all the applause and excitement coming from the squad room, Captain Sullivan opened his door. He shrilled a welcome in his deep Irish brogue.

"Jumpin' Jehoshaphat! I can't believe these tired, sore eyes. If it ain't Dick Tracy and his sidekick Catchem, right back here where it all started. Welcome, Detectives. To what do I owe this pleasure? I haven't got my stack of Irish Sweepstakes tickets to sell yet. Shh!" Snorting and putting his finger to his lips, his face reddened. He was aware as a Police Captain that Irish sweeps were illegal to sell in the U.S. "You can, however, make a donation for the benefit of hospitals in my motherland."

"Good to see you too, Captain," they greeted. "We're back on, looking for the two that got away, Griff and Carol Lynne," Billy continued.

"SABSO received intel on them and the where-a-bouts of the Lynne woman," Johnny said. "It's known that Griff is back in business too."

"SABSO must be glad to have you two for sure. Their intel is far superior to ours. You know how it works on this level; precincts want the collar all to themselves. Enough of that," he waved his hand in dismissal. "We miss you guys. The murder solve rate hasn't been the same since you left. I wish you could come by once in a while and teach these flatfoots some actual detective business. Thankfully, it's my last year," Sullivan touted.

"'Bout time, Captain," Billy murmured.

"Yeah, I agree, Bradshaw. Thirty five years is too long, although I've had a good run," Sullivan boasted.

"Not to mention that fat pension staring you in the mug," Johnny said with sincerity and a slow nod of agreement.

"Just keep in mind, Gentlemen, the only other time you'll get the same kind of reception like when you walked in today will be at your retirement party," Sullivan chuckled.

"Captain, we'd like to use part of the morning roll call to bring the uniforms up to date, if it's all right. I'll take the Detectives, and look at the files," Johnny suggested.

"Be my guest, Detectives," Sullivan said, motioning with a hand gesture to proceed.

"Ahem!" Sullivan cleared his throat, tapping the desk with his finger. "And you thought you'd just walk out, huh?"

Johnny and Billy each lay down a double saw buck on the desk.

"Ah, twenty bucks each. You are gentlemen indeed. Ireland's hospitals thank you. Let me interrupt the squad for you. C'mon."

Chapter 11

"Vero," Johnny answered the phone.

"Ah, glad I got you, Vero. You ain't an easy man to track down these days. I have info for you and Bradshaw," said Captain Sullivan on the other end.

"Shoot, Captain."

"Talk about the luck of the Irish coming my way. You and Bradshaw's seats are still warm from your visit. You're gunna love this, Johnny. Our undercover guys busted a big opium shipment—one of the biggest yet. This one'll boost me into retirement with a bang."

"I'm all ears, Captain," Johnny answered as a matter of rote, but never without thinking of what took place that infamous day at the Devil's door. The Old Brewery building in Chinatown was known as the Labyrinth, named after a myth of ancient Greece. The Labyrinth housed the Minotaur, the monster of Crete, half man and half bull. The Minotaur's invincibility myth ended when the Athenian hero, Theseus, killed it, but Chinatown's Minotaur still existed. Johnny's partially destroyed ear was proof of that.

"Anyway, you remember the trio-Detectives Fang, Chen, and Pan? They're a feather in our cap for sure, Johnny. They raided the opium den on Pearl Street while the delivery was in motion. This bust will make me shine above the other Precincts. That reporter, you remember..." snapping his fingers, trying to remember the name.

"Grace Tilly from The Daily Globe," Johnny finished his thought, hoping never to hear her name again. *Grace knew*

"Yeah, she wants to interview me. Imagine that." Sullivan
gave his hearty signature laugh.

"Me and Bradshaw caught wind of the bust, Captain.
Congratulations! So, who's running the opium dens these
days since we put Mo China behind bars and finally deported
him back to his homeland. I guarantee Chiang Kai-shek will
find him and cut off his balls for cheating the Bureau of
Opium Suppression and skimming money while he lived
here. He's a wanted man."

"That lady Karma is a bitch, ain't she, Vero? He had to
flee China, and he's right back. Don't know who is boss since
he's gone. Anyway, they transferred the opium to a boat right
at the international water line and right into our lap. You
think it's Griff that wised up and stopped at the three-mile
demarcation, staying in international waters?"

"Could be, Captain. I'll get the Coast Guard involved and
see what our intel can muster up. Thanks for the heads up.
That's great news."

"What was that all about, Johnny?" Billy asked.

Johnny gave him the condensed version, filling him in.

"Hmm," was Billy's only comment.

"That's it, hmm? That's all you got, Billy... hmm"?

"I'm surprised we got that much out of him. Usually an
officer in his last year before he retires spends it being a Lame
Duck."

Chapter 12

"She sure is a beauty, don't you say?" Billy asked rhetorically as he ran his hand over the dash of the new 1950 Ford Sedan SABSO provided. "Johnny, where we headed?"

"Fort Wadsworth," Johnny answered.

"Wadsworth Avenue up in Washington Heights?"

"No! F-O-R-T Wadsworth. Staten Island.

"Ah, Commander Fred Cunningham," Billy mumbled.

"Yeah. U.S. Coast Guard Headquarters. Fred's expecting us. He's got some command running the largest Coast Guard operational field on the East Coast. We have to check out the three-mile international water demarcation. Our defrocked ship captain, Griff, knows his shit," Johnny said, filling the conversation.

"Griff has to know, Johnny. You know, all about the waterways and the shipping lanes. After all, he captained a large freighter."

"All that precious cargo he carried got him in trouble, selling off some of it."

"For sure, Billy. We gotta nab this bastard. He's wrecking our city."

Two armed Military Police staffed the guard house. One exited carrying a Thompson submachine gun, nicknamed The Tommy Gun. He walked around the vehicle, giving it a once over while the other guard checked Johnny and Billy's I.D., calling the Commander for clearance.

"Go ahead, Lieutenant, The Commander is expecting you."

Cunningham's office was located a short distance to the water where his Patrol Boat docked, awaiting his beck and call, while all the other Utility Boats patrolled 24/7. His office was military to the tee—everything in its place and a place for everything without a speck of dust. The smell of salt water stood out, giving the overall building a constant musty order.

"Well, I'll be a monkey's uncle. It's been awhile since I've seen you, Lieutenant, and like forever since seeing you—Billy The Kid Bradshaw—in person."

"Ah, that's kind of ya to remember, Fred. That's another lifetime ago," Billy answered kind of shy remembering his days with the Jersey City Giants, the minors for the New York Giants baseball league.

"I'm a hometown guy," the Commander said, "and enjoyed the minor leagues over the majors. It gave the players something to strive and work for–a sense of community and country, if you know what I mean. Too bad about your pitchin' arm. You…"

"Thanks, Commander," Billy interrupted. "That seems a million years and a million tears ago." *He says the same fucking thing every time we see each other. He should record it, so it plays the same spiel.*

"On with it then, Gentlemen. What's the ruckus this time?" Fred asked.

"As we spoke, Fred. Our smuggler, Griff, seems to be back at it and in our… your territory," Johnny pointed out, wanting to be sure Fred was aware who was invading the harbor on his watch.

Good move, getting him riled up, just like we got each other pumped up in the dugout, in-between innings. Billy toed the mark and threw his pitch. "There was a shipment of opium that landed in Captain Sullivan's undercover detective's lap. It was a fluke, Commander,"

"The only fucking fluke I want in these waters, Billy, is the one that don't flounder," Fred said, biting his lip with disdain.

"Now that's one of your better ones, Commander," said Bosun Darby, Commander Cunningham's assistant for years. Everyone chuckled at Fred's lighthearted reference to the fish in his harbor—not wanting Griff's fluke of escaping in the past, having him flounder to catch him.

"Let me show you here," Bosun Darby said, pointing to the map showing the territorial waters of their command.

"It looks like a hop, skip, and a jump from here, Fred," Billy said.

"May be so, Detective," answered Darby, "but the forty-foot Utility Boat traveling at fifteen knots will take approximately twenty minutes. It's deceptive looking at the map. These waters have a life and way of their own, like silhouettes on a shade that can deceive you, Detective."

"Bosun Darby knows these waters as well as your smuggler and I do," Commander Cunningham commented. Billy always thought Darby a weird bird. Something about the Commander's assistant didn't sit right with him.

"When we were on board our ships, I never was privy to that info," Billy said.

"We're ready, Commander. She awaits you."

"Aye, aye, Bosun. Let's roll, Detectives" he grabbed his cap and ushered them to the door. "The last time we were all here, what was it, over a year?" the Commander asked, walking to the dock, eager to board his pride and joy.

"Yeah, time goes by fast, Fred. I can still hear those bullets from Griff's boat guns ricocheting off the metal on your boat that night." Johnny reached for his ear. Memories of the shooting at the old Brewery building that lopped off a piece of his ear still caused phantom pain.

"I didn't have any of them removed. It's a reminder, Johnny. I want this son of a bitch! Now it's our turn."

"You know the routine, Detectives. Life jackets before we cast off." Bosun Darby reminded them, not in a shy way.

Chapter 13

Johnny and Molly had to conduct business as usual in their professional world of police business, outside of their personal lives, living together as lovers.

"Johnny, are you going to use the FBI's expertise and their top undercover lady agent, Leelee Gaye?" Molly's inquiry reflected her unease, not knowing where it came from. *Maybe it was how Johnny felt when my cousin came to visit and I strung him along. Made him think Charlie was an old flame and not my cousin Charlotte nicknamed Charlie.*

"SABSO's got a good handle on it, Molly. Not only do we work hand in hand with the FBI, we also have great relations with Interpol. This agency differs a lot from the NYPD per se."

"I know when my father did a short stint with SABSO before he passed, he wasn't able to say much," Molly pointed out.

"So, you know the drill. Most likely, with this caper, we'll engage our international friends. Remember Inspector Laurent with Interpol?"

"How could any of us forget that crazy serial killer, Jean-Paul Vincent–killing those dance hall girls from the Flamingo Room?"

"Then choosing rooms with certain numbers at the Budapest Hotel because they had biblical meaning to him. My God! Really?" Johnny snorted.

Molly shook her head from side to side. "Tsk, tsk. From what I recall, Laurent was quite an agreeable gentleman when

I spoke to him over the phone. Maybe one day we shall meet." *How about I meet him on our honeymoon to Europe?*

Molly came around her desk, took his left hand in hers. Skillfully manipulating her hand to his ring finger, holding it separate from all the others with a gentle stroke. "See you tonight. Maybe we can talk about you giving up your apartment with Coleman Hawkins."

Johnny felt a rush come over him. He knew discussing that subject of not renewing his lease could cause a knockdown, drag out argument that usually wound up with crazy, hot, make-up sex. But "Hawk," Coleman Hawkins? Her favorite jazz player was always her code for special evenings.

Chapter 14

"Johnny, you know what I've been thinking?" Billy asked, his eyes fixed on the ceiling.

"Sounds like a children's guessing game. Okay, I'll bite. Tell me. If I don't get the right answer, do you become a petulant little brat, or do you win the marbles and go home?"

Billy snickered. "First, what do you think about Carol Lynne being right here under our noses? Yeah, right here in our City. And second, fuck you with your analytical sarcasm."

"Touché. You're right, I'm sorry. Why would you think she's here?"

"Well…Shoeshine Willy had Griff in his chair, correct? That's one. Now add the opium bust that South-Central collared. That's two. Carol Lynne's wire. That's three. They all came within days of each other, correct? One… plus one… plus one," presenting his theory.

"Go ahead, I'm listening."

"How the fuck is that a coincidence? C'mon, Johnny, add it up. Do the math, as Molly says. Now, we have the same scenario we had with our last entanglement with them all. Look, there has to be someone who took Mo China's place in Chinatown, and Sullivan's in the dark who it is. Probably being his last year, along with the huge opium bust to his credit, he doesn't give a shit about finding out or about Alvise LaPoshio's replacement. The Mob's top dog here, allowing all the illegal activity. Who took his place?"

"I get what you're saying, Billy. So, let me ask you… do you think Chinatown and the opium bust has anything to do with us except for getting those two thugs who got away? If SABSO wanted us involved outside of nabbing Griff and Carol Lynne, they would put it on our plate. I don't want that. We have enough to deal with finding that pair. Remember the Chinatown murders ended up totaling eleven and think of how long it took us to get that solved? Both of us almost got killed. Chinatown bosses and the Mott Street Mob are for South-Central and their undercover guys. If we come across any intel while tracking Griff and Carol Lynne, we'll hand it to them on a silver platter, just like Salome gifted the head of John the Baptist to Herod."

"Well, I like my math, Johnny. There have to be ties to Griff and Lynne for them to re-enter the harbor. I don't agree with you. I have this feeling we'll get involved with that bullshit again somewhere along the line during our investigation, regardless of whether we want to. The opium trade all leads down the same path. There must be bread crumbs. I think Carol Lynne is playing us again. I wonder Griff and Carol Lynne are working in concert."

"Like Hansel and Gretel's bread crumbs, huh? You got a point, Partner." Johnny looked thoughtful, reconsidering Billy's one plus one plus one. "You've got a point. Maybe, just maybe…"

Chapter 15

"Hello, this is Warden Nibley."

"Thank you for taking my call, Warden. This is Lieutenant—"

"Yes, I know. My secretary told me," Warden Nibley curtly interrupted.

"You know we're trying to squeeze one of your inmates, Dr. Dean Paul, for information—"

"Oh yes, Lieutenant. I remember your visit," once again interrupting Johnny. "Yes, yes. Dr. Paul has been quite a model prisoner and an asset. I'll miss him, you know."

Is he for real? Johnny wondered, puzzling over the Warden's reply. *What the hell is he flappin' his lips about?*

"What? What do you mean... miss him, Warden?" Johnny asked in surprise.

"Well, I got a call from the Governor about the doctor. You know him. What a fine gentleman, a jolly fellow. We've dined together."

"Warden?" Johnny questioned. *Jolly shit! This ain't Christmas.*

"Well, he told me that there may have been some strings pulled to get the doctor into another...one of those fancier gated communities," which was Nibley's way of saying a prison that has fewer restrictions on its inmates. "You know, Detective, where he can be in a single cell away from the general population and all. I believe it was your suggestion. I heard there might even be a program he's going to teach to help the inmates get some sort of education. You boys in

SABSO know how to pull strings," Warden Nibley said in his cavalier English, applying a contemptuous sense to an overbearing swashbuckler.

"Go ahead, Lieutenant, I apologize for my interruptions. State your reason for calling."

"As I started to say Warden, we are trying to find the whereabouts of his fiancé, Carol Lynne, who's still at large. He's been cooperating with us. On my last visit, he gave us information from her letters that lead us to look to where she may be hiding out. I just wanted to check if he got any mail since our last visit. We wanted, Warden, to check the postmarks."

"Of course. Can you hold on, Lieutenant? I'll have my secretary check the mail roster." Warden Nibley offered without allowing Johnny the opportunity to answer.

"Hello, Detective. This is the Warden's secretary. There has been no mail to inmate Dean Paul, number three-three-three-two-four, since your last visit. Is there anything else?" she asked.

Not knowing what the hell just happened or why Nibley didn't get back on the line, Johnny mumbled his answer. "N-n-no thank you. Thank the Warden, will you?"

"Good day, Detective."

Johnny heard the click and lay the phone in its cradle.

Billy grinned with raised eyebrows. "Johnny, you look like you just stepped in dog shit in the middle of your living room rug, wondering how it got there since you don't have a dog."

Chapter 16

The happy foursome had a wonderful night filled with laughter, flirting, wining, and dining at *Delmonico's*. Lola DuBoise, the incredible Jazz singer who rocked Variety's tabloid as the top Jazz entertainer in New York City at *The No It Awl Jazz Club,* entertained them following drinks and dancing.

They never talked shop on the rare or special occasions outside the traditional holiday or birthday celebrations presented themselves. Nancy would not understand the special jargon law enforcement uses in their everyday chatter or the precarious situations they encountered. Billy rarely brought his work home. Nancy didn't want to live in fear of Billy's safety. She often relived that infamous day Johnny lost part of his ear in a shootout. Nancy knew that bullet or any other one could have Billy's name on it. Molly knew the drill and respected and understood her civilian friend's wishes and fears, for she too knew the dangers Johnny faced each day.

****

The couples took separate taxi's home to keep the night young and flavorful–filled with spice and everything nice.

*Showing mercy to those shipwrecked
is not a fickle mistress.*

Chapter 17

Sunday mornings weren't so fancy. Molly always enjoyed a stroll along the Turtle Gardens Walkway beside the East River. The skyline was magnificent with an unobstructed view of the United Nations Building. Periodically, taking a break from walking arm-in-arm, Johnny and Molly sat on one of the park benches to enjoy the sounds and smells, and people watched.

"You know, Molly, any of these people walking by could turn out to be Carol Lynne."

"And Griff will be by her side," Molly laughed. "I think I might have to side with Billy on this one. It's possible, Miss. Lynne is right in front of our noses. Look at this City, Johnny. Look out there," Molly said, sweeping her hand in an arc. "She could be anywhere, or as you said, walking right here. She played us all those months we hunted her. She knows how to manipulate; she's devious; and she is a killer. What did she say in her wire to you? 'She has an insurance policy,' that she believes will get her what she wants? A deal? It wouldn't surprise me to learn she's planning her fiancé's escape. Maybe this insurance policy she's holding will help secure that. You must remember the infamous bank robber, Harry "the Horse" Fuller?"

"How could any of us forget? His buddies gave him that nickname because his face was as long as a horse's. It's rumored he got that way from spending every day at the track." They both laughed.

"And that's why he robbed banks, to support his horse racing and gambling addictions. His escape from prison was masterful. He held a guard hostage with a fake gun. He carved it from a bar of soap and colored it with shoe polish." Molly returned to their nemesis. "Carol Lynne is masterful too. I wouldn't put anything past her. She's not a common lover—untrustworthy or whimsical. She is smart, manipulative, and cunning, like I've said before."

"I'd like to quote you by saying one plus one always equals two. I can't dismiss what you and Billy are saying, but I'll have to give this a lot of thought. She just might try to spring the Doc. It all adds up now. I spoke with Warden Nibley. He told me Dr. Paul is getting his transfer orders from the Governor."

"Johnny, we knew it would happen in exchange for his cooperation. It's just happening sooner than we expected."

"The pieces of the puzzle are coming together."

"What do you mean? How?"

"When Billy and I visited the prison and saw Dr. Paul, we told him we checked the mail roster. He said he got plenty of letters and we knew they were from his fiancé. We thought we called his bluff. We didn't check the roster, but he didn't care if we saw the list. He knew what we were looking for. They had this all worked out between them, knowing he would get moved in exchange for the letters from Carol Lynne. He gave us those letters too fast. He knew we would look at the postmarks and figure she was in Northern Italy. He hoped we would go there and his transfer to a new location would come through while me and Billy were in Europe. In a facility with less stringent security, Carol Lynne would help him escape. That conniving son of a bitch. They anticipated our hand before we played it. Those two are—"

"Deceitful manipulators who kill people? They'd make great poker players. They're playing us again. I think you, Billy, and SABSO have your work cut out for you. Like Billy, I think Carol Lynne is here... close to Dr. Paul. You're wondering how she or the Doc got those letters mailed from Italy, aren't you? And, was she really there or do they have an accomplice? It's not a complicated ploy; it's simple."

"Hmm," Johnny hummed. "Simple how, Molly?"

"I remember my parents used a little-known fact since we came from Italy, you'll remember."

"How can I forget? I see the Italian in you click its heels now and then. Go ahead."

"I knew you were working on the theory that she has an accomplice, and it was a sure thing. I never gave it a second thought until now."

"Well—"

"She could have used a private mailing service."

"What the hell. I never gave that a thought."

"Italy reformed its postal organization by Royal Decree, which gave way to the Directorate General of Posts and Telegraphs, which separated from the Ministry of Public Works. It became the Ministry of Posts and Telegraphs. That was what my parents would use. It established offices to process mail and telegrams among other services, and both send and receive. Maybe—"

"She used that," Johnny finished. "Son of a bitch!"

"As I was about to say, she could have left the letters at the Ministry of Posts and pre-paid with instructions to mail them at certain times. One hundred thousand Lira would persuade a postal employee to do a lot of things."

"Holy shit!" Johnny exclaimed.

"Simmer down. One hundred thousand Lira is only about a hundred bucks," Molly explained.

"Jesus, I was going to say if it was that kind of money, I'd jump at the hundred thousand number. I thought it was a hundred grand."

"This transfer of Dr. Dean Paul is going to happen, but we need to slow it down. I'll get to work on it in the morning. This is a bone of contention for all of us again, Johnny," Molly's half smile showed she had a plan in mind.

"What do you mean? Who is all of us?"

"You, Billy, SABSO, me, and now South-Central since they have the opium collar, and Griff and Lynne are still at large. What do *they* say? All roads lead to Rome. Let's go home," Molly said, changing the subject. "We never finished our conversation."

"What conversation?" Johnny asked.

"The one about you giving up your north end Manhattan apartment," she said with a smirk.

Chapter 18

Johnny stepped up into an empty chair at Willy's Shoeshine before heading to the SABSO office. The directory listing in the lobby simply said NYC Police Task Force, not Sabre Blue Society.

Willy readied his stand for business each day by seven AM when security unlocked the lobby doors to the Feed House. Johnny was usually right behind.

"Good morning, Willy. Give me the usual, will ya?" Johnny greeted.

"Yes sir, Detective. I see you got yourself a new pair of them Florsheim's you like. Must have set you back a few. Where's that partner of yours? Ain't be seein' him since your last visit. Be sure to tell him what ol' Willy says, ya know; you can tell a lot 'bout a man that has a shine—"

"On his shoes and those that ain't," Johnny said, continuing Willy's saying.

"Sure is fact," both finished in unison, laughing.

"I'll tell him, Willy. You have anything? Any word on the street about that ugly guy, Griff? How about who's running Chinatown?" Johnny asked.

"Why don't you just ask me who's runnin' at Aqueduct Race Track and who the winner's gunna be in the third, ya know?" Willy chuckled.

"If anyone knows, it's you, Willy."

"Well, tell my bookmaker, will you, Detective? If rollin' them dice didn't give me so much trouble way back."

"Willy, stay with the Daily Racing Form. We don't want to go down that road for sure."

"Good advice, Detective. You saved me, knowin' I was innocent and never killed nobody at that dice game. If it weren't for you, I'd still be in prison. I keep you in my prayers, Lieutenant. Well, let me see now. I did hear somethin' 'bout runnin' the gamblin' in Chinatown. I'm glad my bookie ain't with them. Those Chinamen are a mean bunch over there, ya know, Detective? I heard they brought this guy in to keep everybody in line and pick up what those murders you had to deal with lost 'em. Man alive, Lieutenant, I don't know how you do it, ya know? Lookin' at all those dead people, don't ya know."

"You get used to it, Willy. It's like you grow up and your fear of the dark goes away. Since they can't tell you who killed them, I become a voice for them."

"I'm still afraid of the dark." Willy's shoulders drooped. He hung his head, pretending to look at the shoes he was shining. "Yes sir, those Chinamen they a mean bunch. I heard they cut off three fingers of some guy that was cheatin' at the card table, ya know." Willy looked around to be sure nobody else was listening to their conversation.

"Willy, that's not my problem. I need solid information and you've been my man."

"Well, Lieutenant, there's this here fella, ya know. My bookie tells me he got to give all his play slips to him now. Somethin' new, ya know. So, when and if I win, its gunna take a few more days to get paid, ya know. To me, that's bullshit, ya know. But I don't have a choice. I've been playin' with my bookie for years now. We know each other, ya know?"

"Willy, these shoes are going to be the envy of my squad," Johnny said in a voice that carried and handed Willy his usual ten spot far above the cost of a shine. "Keep the change and your ears open. I need something concrete."

"Yes, sir. One pocket for the wife and one pocket for my bookie. God bless you, Lieutenant. My eyes and ears are workin' overtime, ya know."

Chapter 19

"Johnny, did you see this morning headlines?" Billy asked, throwing the Daily Globe onto his desk.

"I must have missed it when I stopped at Willy's."

"I should see Willy; I need a shine."

ANOTHER CHINATOWN HUGE OPIUM BUST
RUINING OUR CITY!
HOW WILL OUR BOYS IN BLUE TAKE DOWN
THE NEW BOSS OF CHINATOWN?

By Grace Tilly
Story page six

"What? She's at it again. That broad won't quit," Johnny said, reading the headline.

"Whatta you gonna do, anything?" Billy asked with a sigh.

"Not a goddamn thing. That's South-Central's case and Grace belongs to whoever wants to grab onto her skirt. I let go, remember?"

"I do, but you realize Molly will see this too."

"I'm done with Grace. Molly and I are...well..." Johnny stammered.

"What? Getting serious?"

"I have that feeling again. This is the only time since Simone that I think I may be in over my head... I *might be* in love."

"Does Molly know?" Billy asked, giving a hearty chuckle before he moved on to business. "So, I guess Willy doesn't have any news, but Grace does. I wonder who else knows who is the new boss of Chinatown."

"I'm going with your theory, okay? A new Chinatown Boss, and it seems there's a new Boss over all the operations too... most likely who ever took over Mott Street. Another hand signal from Ralph "the Trucker" Mariozo and his cousin Jimmy "the Rat" Enrizzi. As Molly says; 'their hands reach out of the grave.' I guess we're gonna get involved. Goddamn it!"

"It won't be so bad. We're aware of their inner workings. They won't change a lot as long as their operation is still running. It's just like changing oil in the car... smooth, out with the old and in with the new. Whatta you have there?" Billy asked.

"I stopped by South-Central before I hit Willy's. It's the Carol Lynne jacket."

"Let's have a look. Toss it here, will you? Oh yeah! Looky, looky. Dr. Paul admitted she helped with cover-ups at the M.E.'s office of people they killed. We also know she can disguise herself. That fiasco at the airport was insane. It's all here. She murdered the female police officer, took her uniform—"

"Don't forget the squad car she stole and the wigs we found at her house," Johnny added.

"I remember. They found the burned-out car up in the Bronx at Van Courtland Park. Look here. Dr. Paul told us she used an alias on her passport that was pretty clever—Lorac

Sreknoy, Carol Yonkers spelled backward. What do you think happened to her house in Yonkers? And the police uniform she stole."

"Who knows? It was her parent's house, but that's a good question. We should check the records to see if it is still in her mother's name and who's paying the taxes. Her M.O. is obvious. She wants something, but what? Pro quid pro. Something to trade for Monica's journal, her insurance policy."

"Her behavior may flip-flop in other things, but not her love for Dr. Paul. She's sure loyal to him. Those love letters were steamy. I think their love is real. I believe she wants him to be free so they can do their thing." Billy's thought resonated.

"Oh yeah. Killing's their thing."

Au Courant...
A French expression meaning
well-informed

Chapter 20

"Vero here," Johnny answered his phone.

"It's Molly. We… I really mean me and I guess South-Central… just got a tip about who the new Bosses are. I realize it's our fiasco, but I couldn't wait until tonight to tell you. This may give you a heads up as to how SABSO will deal with this insane woman, Carol Lynne. My office got called to a triple homicide at Chatham Square. No, it was not the Tongs or The On Leong gangs. It was a professional hit. All three were on their knees, their hands tied behind their backs, and all shot in the back of the head. No shell casings. During all my career, I have not witnessed a triple murder scene."

"The hit man used a revolver? … Probably a .22 caliber. That makes it up close and personal to be sure. Thanks, Molly, there's always a first for everything, you know that. It looks like you and your people will be busy. This tells me that it's starting all over again. Three hits soon after the opium raid and hearing Griff is back."

"Let's not forget your Teletype from Miss Lynne. Here we go again, Johnny. I just hope they don't tally up another eleven murders. Anyway, here are the new Bosses: Qin Shi Ming and Vito "Mad Dog" Vaccaro. I don't see SABSO out of the loop here."

"I'll run the names and see what comes up on them both. They're new names to me."

"Us too, Johnny. See you tonight."

"I heard part of what you were saying. Clue me in, will ya?"

"You heard the names of the new Bosses? Here, I wrote them down. Let's run them through SABSO's system and see what it spits out. These names seem to have meanings to them. Why is this Vito Vaccaro called "Mad Dog?" Johnny wondered.

"I'll run them. Maybe we'll get a hit. Don't forget, we're up for transporting the Judge. We gotta get out of this detail."

"He put a lot of people away, Billy. There must be a who's who list of perps who want him knocked off, including Ralph "The Trucker" and Jimmy "The Rat's" people. It was Judge Delbert Millhouse that put them away."

"Give that information to research. Maybe when we get back, we'll have some answers regarding these unknowns. Let's go escort His Honor."

Chapter 21

"Judge, your escorts are here," the Bailiff's voice echoed into the Judge's chambers.

"Hello, Detectives. I'm ready; shall we go?" Judge Millhouse said, stuffing a few things into his pockets. "Can't forget my pipe, boys."

Judge Delbert Millhouse was a stout man, bold, strong-minded, and vigorous. His Honor, although raised on a dairy farm in upstate New York, oozed city slicker. He always dressed fashionably, wearing his trademark bow ties with wide suspenders that buttoned to his pants to keep them up despite his protruding beer belly. He loved the law. He embellished his decisions to those that stood before him in his courtroom with details and fine points, always making the sentence more interesting and entertaining by adding extra details. He decreed harsh sentences prescribed by law with such grace that adjudged criminals would thank him.

His Honor's driver parked his car curb side at the scheduled time the Judge preferred. A uniformed New York City Police Sergeant drove the car and stood diligently awaiting his boss.

Johnny and Billy walked on each side of the Judge, quickly moving him down the long row of steps to the sidewalk. Out of the corner of his eye, Billy caught sight of a man approaching too fast. Billy's suspicion grew, and he warned Johnny, yelling, "gun, gun." Billy pushed the Judge into the back seat, covering him with his own body.

Johnny and the Judge's driver drew their revolvers, firing at the man who attempted to assassinate the Honorable Delbert Millhouse. The thwarted assassin fell to his knees with his gun in one hand, grabbing his wounds with the other. Johnny took the gun from him and bent, trying to hear his mumbling.

"Who sent you?" Johnny demanded, laying him down.

"Get me a priest," he whispered.

A fucking button man with religion? "Don't die without forgiveness. Why did you want to kill the Judge? I'll tell the priest you were repentant. Somebody call a priest," Johnny yelled to convince the man who lay dying,

"Tell me who sent you. The priest is on his way. Tell me before it's too late or he won't be able to help you redeem your soul. Stay with me; the Sergeant just told me the priest will be here any moment to give you your last rites. Don't waste your opportunity. Tell me why you wanted to kill the Judge. Who sent you to kill him?" Johnny applied pressure on the wound with handkerchiefs passed to him. He appealed to the wounded man's conscience, trying to keep him alive until he confessed his guilt to save his soul and gave up the name of the man who sent him.

A dozen policemen appeared on the scene within minutes and swept the Judge away. Billy came to Johnny's side and kneeled, trying to hear what the dying man might say.

"See, the priest is here," Johnny said, pointing at Billy.

Without missing a beat, Billy bent closer. All his Roman Catholic schooling and service as an altar boy flooded his mind. "Tell me, my son. What is your confession? Why did you want to kill Judge Millhouse?" Billy recited, "In the name of the Father, the Son and…" making the sign of the cross on the dying man's chest. "Through this holy rite may the Lord…"

"Vee, vee," he whispered.

"Who is Vee?" Johnny asked as Billy continued his charade.

"Our Father who art in heaven…"

"Vee, Veet," he gasped, his voice weakening.

"Was it, Vito, my son?" Billy asked in a calm murmur.

He sighed, "Yes, Fath…er."

"He's gone, Johnny. Let him go," Billy said.

Word spread throughout the Feed House. Police swarmed the area, pushing back the crowd.

Johnny looked up. Pale and trembling, Molly reached for his hand. He climbed to his feet and she pulled him close.

Chapter 22

An anxious day can end much better…

****

"Johnny, you and Billy… really?" Molly stated sarcastically.

"I know. It was a last-minute change in venue for the Judge's escort. We were immediately available. What the hell, we couldn't say no to a free lunch with the most prominent judge in New York, the Honorable Delbert Millhouse, soon to be nominated to the Supreme Court. What a privilege and an opportunity!"

"I know what I feel is hideous and is part and parcel of your position with SABSO, considering everything else that goes on—terrorists, our enemy infiltrating our shore line. By the way, what did you find out about going to the three-mile demarcation with Fred Cunningham?" Molly asked, not in a happy tone.

"Wow! Nothing gets by you, Molly," Johnny said.

"Are you surprised? You'd better be careful," she answered with a sly grin. She continued in a more serious tone. "You're cleared of the shooting. No Grand Jury. I met with His Honor in chambers when he insisted on returning to the courtroom. He's diligent in his support of our law enforcement. No one will challenge his decision."

"Thank you. Anything to avoid that fiasco," Johnny said with a sigh.

"Anything?" Molly questioned with lust on her mind. "I'll be right back. Pour us a drink and put on the "Hawk," she purred in her persuasive sexy voice.

Chapter 23

The SABSO system hit on the two names—Qin Shi Ming and Vito Vaccaro. Johnny studied the printout.

"These reports should be on *The Hit Parade* radio show. Here, read this," Johnny said, handing it to Billy.

"Hmm. Just like I said. Changing the oil on your car; out with the old and in with the new… smooth. I wish we woulda had our fingertips on this at South-Central. It would have saved us days of gumshoe. Dig this. Qin means a dynasty that built the Great Wall. Shi Ming means to become blind with a mission, a set task. If you ask me, building the Great Wall of China was some fucking task!"

"So, I guess someone sent him here on a mission. He's to be blind to everything but whatever it takes to complete the task—build something great."

"I'd guess that something great is a Chinatown Empire under the control of Vito "Mad Dog" Vaccaro."

"And what do you make of his sheet?" Johnny urged Billy to continue.

"Vito's jacket is pages of felony charges. Like Alvise LaPoshio, no convictions."

"We still can't tell shit from Shinola on Griff or Carol Lynne." Johnny's annoyance was obvious. "And what kind of name is Griff? Is it a nickname, his first name, part of a name? Only having that by itself, we've never been able to run a search against it."

"Oh, I just remembered. Look at this," Billy said, ignoring Johnny's complaint about Griff. He handed him a report on the Carol Lynne house in Yonkers.

"Nice. So, the house is in a Trust. The Trustee pays the property taxes and utilities. The Trustee is Carol Lynne? She has full control, and continues to maintain it. It says here that Lynne's parents became wealthy selling minerals and materials to the highest bidder during the War. Sound familiar?"

"Sure as shit, Johnny. That ties in with Griff selling Bauxite he stole from the freighters he captained and selling to the highest bidder. That, in turn, caused him to lose his captain's license. There has to be a tie-in. For sure Griff and Lynne know each other. Both of them are working the same scam. That's no coincidence."

"I bet they found out it was better to join forces than compete against each other—better odds."

"Being united would give them a powerful hold on the market they're dealing in; you know, edge out the competition. Now we know the rest of the story," Billy said with confidence.

"If Lynne's parents were as ruthless as their daughter, they could have committed murder or knocked off any competition for the fortune that this report mentions."

"Johnny, that day with the Judge—" Billy switched to the incident that bothered him.

"You were great. We work well together as a team, and have for years, but the assassin's dying confession--mumbling and not saying the full name and all--according to Molly, didn't produce what we needed to bring charges. We know who he was referring to." Johnny didn't skip a beat, returning to their investigation.

I guess we did the right thing. Impersonating a priest poked Billy's Catholic conscience before he came back to Lynne and Griff.

"Now we're back on track with these two. This info really ties them together. I wonder how tight they actually are… or were, if you catch my drift," Billy mused.

"She's too smart to get involved with just anyone. Although she could do a one off to make a deal. With the wealth they accumulated, there had to be payoffs and corruption, just like Griff did to get into the harbor."

"True, but there's no way, no how, to get deep into that after so many years," Billy said. "Payoffs and information disappear; people die off. I hope you're not thinking of going down that rabbit hole."

"Maybe later, not now. Imagine what we might uncover—espionage, murders, love triangles, foreign dignitaries, payoffs—"

"Slow down, buddy; come back to reality. Sounds like it would make a great novel."

"Yeah, but the thought won't go away. You're right," Johnny sighed. "Let's get to what's on our plate here. The three-mile international waters gave us a good perspective of what Griff is doing now to avoid capture. It costs him more to employ smaller boats to meet him out there, but he can get the opium and women to shore without detection, mostly. I'm not giving up on the idea that Griff and Lynne are in cahoots. After reading this report, they have to be."

"Facts are facts, Johnny. The puzzle pieces are coming together. The new Chinatown Bosses are secondary for us, but they got to be first for Molly and South-Central."

There is no absence of malice.

Chapter 24

"Let's take a ride to Yonkers. We can meet with someone in the Trust Department at the bank about the Lynne Trust, ask some questions, and do another walk-through in the Lynne house—take our time," Johnny said, getting up to move out.

"Wait a minute. Is that last search warrant still good? We can surely tap into Judge Millhouse. I don't know what you think, but he owes us big time as far as I'm concerned."

"I gotcha covered. We probably could still ride that warrant. However, we can use exigent circumstances. I think we can argue this situation requires action to forestall the imminent escape of a suspect or destruction of property. We believe Carol Lynne is here, and she'll return to destroy evidence before running."

"Sounds like we've got double trouble covered," Billy snickered.

****

Billy used his hook-pick-pin set and jimmied the lock with precision, opening the back door with ease. He crouched to be sure none of the neighbors were hanging laundry or mowing their lawns. They didn't want to raise suspicion and alert the Yonkers Police to a break-in in progress. They had to be on the QT. He signaled Johnny in the car, quickly entering the house.

"I wonder if the Yonkers uniforms still patrol this house. Whatta ya think, Johnny?"

"Nah. Not these days. Maybe a cruiser for the whole street once in a blue moon. If they do, they won't recognize our car. Why would they be here? No reason. Start looking deep. Whatever we move, put back exactly like you found it."

"I don't know what we will find. We gave this place a going over once before," Billy insisted.

"Shh! Billy. Listen. There's someone knocking at the door. Shit! Get down."

Billy slowly depressed the slat on the blinds. "Holy shit, Johnny, it's the cops. Do you believe it? I feel like a kid when we hid from the cops after we turned the fire hydrants on in the summer," he said with a slight laugh. "The cop is talking to a woman, probably a neighbor. She must have thought she saw something. Well, I'll be a monkey's uncle."

"What do you see?" Johnny questioned.

"The cops are getting back into the patrol car. They're probably calling it in as a false alarm because," he chuckled, "the lady has a beer in her hand. I'll bet they think she's on the sauce and seeing things. She's still staring at the house, but they just pulled away."

"That was fun; keep looking. There has to be something we overlooked when we were here last time."

"I'm going up in the attic," Billy said, giving Johnny a heads-up.

Johnny heard shuffling noises overhead—Billy stepping off the pull-down ladder, cursing at the cobwebs, as he brushed them away. Johnny explored the bedroom.

"I found something. C'mon up here."

"Whatta ya have, partner?"

"Watch your head stepping off the ladder. Look at this panel. It looked off center, so I pushed on it." Billy pulled boxes from under the eaves and brushed dust off the lids.

"Good work. How the fuck did we miss this? We were here, what? Two, three times with Yonkers uniforms searching this place," Johnny said.

"Don't matter. They're just boxes filled with files, papers, and shit. I guess we should look through it though. … This is interesting. These appear to be ledgers. I wish it was Monica's journal. Then we could tell Miss Lynne to go fuck herself."

"Wishful thinking. Let's take the boxes with us. We'll look through them back at the Feed House. There's nothing else here that looks like anything. Take a gander and see if the neighbor is still looking at the window while I go out to the garage. I can't figure out why the garage is separate from the house and you have to drive your car in from the alley behind the house. Crazy!"

"No, she's not there any longer," Billy said. "Probably went for another beer. I hope she doesn't pop out of the bushes when we leave. We'll go out the front. Her house faces the door we came in. Wow! Imagine two NYC Detectives with The Sabre Blue Society, having full authority, tiptoeing around like teenagers pulling a prank on a neighbor. Now, this is something I will have to tell Angie for our future grandkids. But she can't tell Molly."

Johnny made his way to the garage. When he returned to the house, he called out.

"I'm right here," Billy answered. "What the hell?" He reached for his gun.

"No, no, I'm good. Do you remember what the YPD said was in the garage when everyone submitted their findings?" he asked.

"I do. YPD said there was a Chevy coupe and two drums. Are they still there?"

"Well, the Chevy coupe must have flown the coop. But the two drums? I thought they were part of a drum set that you play."

"Aren't they?" Billy waited for the shoe to drop.

"They're drums alright. But not the kind you play. There are two fifty-five-gallon drums. I couldn't even tilt 'em, they're so fuckin' heavy."

"Are you thinking what I'm thinking?"

"Bet your bottom dollar, Billy. Get YPD to hightail it back here on the double. I can't believe they would have—"

"The old lady is out again with another beer, and here's the patrol car. Let's cut 'em off at the pass and shut this nosy Parker up." Billy opened the door, flashed his badge, and told the woman to stay put as he approached the YPD. Three patrol cars parked on the street with flashing lights, surprising him. *Jesus, I hate when they keep the lights on. It draws all the fuckin' neighbors.*

"I'm Captain Brodsky. We haven't met, Lieutenant Vero." He studied Johnny's credentials, touting NYPD Special Task Force. "Why are you both back here? This is Yonkers jurisdiction." Brodsky came off all territorial, and Johnny hoped he didn't want to engage in a pissing match.

"Well, Captain, we have the original search warrant which still holds. We don't want to step on anyone's toes. We're working on that missing person who escaped, Carol Lynne. She lived here. If you check, you will see she's on the FBI's most wanted and Interpol's list. This was her mother's house and—"

"I remember it very well, Lieutenant. Too well, if you ask me. The whole story put Yonkers on the map. We had patrol here twenty-four seven for months. I hope we don't have that scenario again. Our budget is ripping at the seams now."

"As I was about to say, Captain, we found something in the garage that most likely will be your crime scene. Sorry, it'll probably stretch your men for a while."

"Mother of God! Help me make retirement," Brodsky mumbled. "Lead the way, Lieutenant."

Johnny walked the path to the garage, passing the neighbor who was speaking with the other uniforms. He heard her say, "That's him right there. Arrest him."

"There's always one," Brodsky muttered under his breath.

"We… I mean NYPD… never looked in the garage because your uniforms were with us. They took that area. Their report says there was a Chevy Coupe and two drums. We didn't look into it, thinking what they meant was two instruments—drums that you play. Take a look, Captain." Johnny waited for his response.

"Jesus, Mary, and Joseph," he mumbled, making the sign of the cross and pushing his hat off his brow. "That's two fuckin' drums for sure. Wait 'till I get my hands on those guys. I can assure you—"

"Never mind that. I see your opinion is the same as mine."

Captain Brodsky was in a fury, ordering his men to get hammers and crowbars from their squad cars.

The cops worked diligently to pry open the two tightly sealed drums. When the first one popped open, the stench drove them all back. They buried their noses in their suit jacket sleeves.

"Oh my God! Stop! Don't open the other one. Good God! It's a… part of a body. What the hell is that liquid? Quick… cover it up! You're right, Lieutenant

; this is now my crime scene. Seal off this place, boys, and put a guard on the garage. Let's get a truck here. Start questioning that nosy neighbor. I want to know about the people who lived here. Jesus Christ! Lieutenant, I didn't mean to come off—"

"It's all good, Captain. I'd like a complete report from any autopsy performed, that is, if the M.E. can do one. Doesn't look promising."

****

Back in the car, Billy asked Johnny to get the Vicks VapoRub[3] from the glove compartment.

"Can't get that gawd awful smell out of your nose, eh, Billy?"

"I don't know how you do it. The smell of death just lingers."

They finally made their way to the bank, eager to see the Lynne Trust document.

"I'm sorry, Detectives. You should know I cannot show you any records or files unless you have a subpoena duces tecum."

"Thank you, Miss. Crenshaw. We'll be back, but for now we will abide by your rules," Johnny answered.

"Not mine, Detective. The rules of Law." Her snide reply accompanied a fake smile.

"I guess we've met a Philadelphia lawyer." Billy's snarky remark disclosed his annoyance.

---

3 Crime-scene detectives report that a dab of *VapoRub* under the nose helps block obnoxious odors.

Chapter 25

Johnny and Billy returned to the Feed House eager to look into the ledgers recovered from the Lynne attic. After some digging, they discovered references to shipments of stolen minerals, including Bauxite, as to who, what and where it all went down.

"Holy shit, Johnny. It's all here in these ledgers. Time, places and code names for everybody who did business together. This is that rabbit hole you wanted to go down in the near future."

"Fuck the future, Billy. What does it say? Let me see."

Billy handed him a ledger.

"Very interesting. My God! How did we miss these?"

"It doesn't matter. We have 'em now, don't we?"

"Those fuckin' code names again. What is it with these people?"

"It's in code so if and when they get caught, their identities are secret," Billy said. "They're not supposed to know who they're dealing with. We can decipher this. Tell me the code names."

"Okay. Listen: HQ, Aussies, G-scar, NYKings, Minors. It lists all the transactions by dates, locations, transfers from who to who. These deals go back to 1942 and stop in 1945. All during the War. These bastards were selling whatever minerals they could get their hands on to the highest bidder, even if it was to our enemy."

"Like I said before. If the Lynne family is wealthy, Griff should be too, if he was in on it."

"I don't know, Billy. Let's break these code names. We certainly can figure who G-scar is. Has to be Griff. NYKings must have been during the time of Ralph "the Trucker" and his cousin, Jimmy "the Rat." Who, though, are the Aussies, and who are the Minors? Let's run what we have—the minerals and the code names—through SABSO. Let's see what the computer comes up with."

"Ten four; I'm on it. What about HQ? We really need to get on Dr. Paul and squeeze him. Do you think HQ is the Lynne family?"

"How can we pressure Paul? He's in prison. Not much we can do from here, except…"

"What? I know that look, Johnny."

"Molly said she can have the Governor delay the paperwork to stall Dr. Paul's move. During that time, we can push him for more information on all this."

"Do you think he's privy to the information in these ledgers?" Billy asked.

"It's worth a shot, don't you think?"

"Anything is worth a shot. You of all people should know that. It was Dr. Paul who took that shot at us, hoping it would find its mark and kill at least one of us."

"You're right, Billy. It's worth a shot. I want that shot back. I want to recapture that day Dr. Paul almost killed us and I want a shot to pin their asses to the wall."

Chapter 26

Johnny and Billy entered the Feed House lobby, cautiously aware of their surroundings since Shoeshine Willy said Griff was in his chair asking about cops' comings and goings.

"You pressed the button to Molly's floor, not ours," Billy pointed out, entering the elevator.

"I want to run this by Molly. Go get the ledgers and bring them to her office. Besides, we have to talk about Dr. Paul's next move… I mean our next move to slow his transfer."

****

"Miss Penett, Lieutenant Vero is here," Molly's secretary announced him over the intercom.

"Send him in, Louise. Thank you."

"Johnny, I know we didn't have time this morning, but here, right now?" Molly teased with a suggestive smile. Their eyes locked in a shared pensive moment before the intercom buzzed. "Detective Bradshaw is here."

"There goes our chance."

"There's always later, Molly."

"Send him in. Hold my calls, Louise."

"Molly, is the FBI… I mean is Agent Bollinger from the Chinatown murders being called in again for the triple you told me about?"

"Not yet, Lieutenant," using his formal address in her office even though their living arrangements weren't as secret as they thought. According to Louise, the entire fifth floor knows it.

"Just a thought, Molly; just a thought before the investigation gets out of hand again. We have a lot to share with you and your people. Sooner or later, you'd find it out, so now's as good a time as any."

"Is that what those dusty books you're holding are all about, Detective Bradshaw?" Molly inquired.

"Yeah, sort of." Billy said.

"Okay, Detective, let's see this 'sort of' you're speaking about." Molly picked one up, then another, thumbing through them all, one by one. "It looks like a jumble with entries representing times, places, and look at this… initials," she said in surprise. "Now that's interesting. So, let's see for an example," Molly pointed, moving her finger across the page to each column. "It says G-scar had a delivery to NYKings on nine twenty, forty-three. Pickup Aussie. What is this, and where did you get these?" Molly questioned.

"It's… you know," Billy answered, ducking his head, not meeting her eyes.

"I get it, Detective. But you know and I know that I will bring these ledgers into evidence. I hope you obtained them legally. I am well aware how some things happen in this business. I assume you and or SABSO have this 'sort of' figured out," Molly smirked, glancing at Billy.

"We do, Molly," Johnny answered, "both how we discovered them and the information in them. We think that G-scar is Griff; NYKings are Ralph "the Trucker" Mariozo and Jimmy "the Rat" Enrizzi; Aussie is Australia; and Minors are the underlings that Ralph and Jimmy put in charge. Now Qin Shi Ming, the new Chinatown Boss, took Mo China's place, and Vito "Mad Dog" Vaccaro is the new Boss who took

Alvise LaPosio's place on Mott Street. You remember why Griff lost his freighter ship captain's license—"

"Sure. He stole some mineral from the shipments and sold it," Molly recalled.

"Aussie, I mean Australia, is the largest producer of Bauxite, the mineral Griff sold. It's aluminum-rich and was in demand for the War efforts. His original country, Guyana, ranked among the top ten producers of the stuff. So, all of them—Griff, Mariozo, Enrizzi, Mo China, LaPosio, and the Lynnes—were tied together in this scheme, including our person of interest, Carol Lynne. Her parents got wealthy from their participation. We think her parents masterminded this lucrative scheme. That's how the Lynne woman is able to travel. Her parents left her a sizeable trust fund. The bank won't release any records without—"

"I know, Detective, a subpoena duces tecum. I can get that for you without any questions, if you want it," Molly answered, interrupting Johnny. "This is great intel, Detectives. I think I—"

"Keep it under your hat, Molly. This doesn't go any further than your desk at this moment," Johnny stated with a death stare.

"We're good, Detectives."

They knew they could trust Molly to keep the information under wraps, both as their friend and in her position as D.A. What they didn't know was if and how she could be an asset to their case.

"Finding who the Minors are will help all of us: my office, South-Central, and SABSO," Molly said.

"Just like the baseball Minors, Molly, players who aren't ready for the big leagues. We kinda figure them to be out of all of this: the dock bosses, the Chinatown Boss, and, of course, The Mott Street Boss," Billy added.

"Okay, we know who they all are, but something is missing. It has to be right in front of us, but not talking to us. How about this, Detectives? What or who is the connection between the Dock Boss and our new Chinatown Boss, Qin Shi Ming? Because there's no one in between Qin Shi and the top dog, Vito "Mad Dog" Vaccaro," Molly said.

"There could be. I like that," Johnny said.

"How about you, Detective?" Molly turned to Billy.

"Sure, why not? We've got nothin' to lose. I'll go along with your theory, Molly. The million-dollar question is whose feet fill those shoes?"

"Maybe if we see it in front of us. I'll list them on the board," Molly said, dragging the blackboard over from the adjoining conference room.

"Here we are, gentlemen." Molly's chalk squealed as she wrote, sending a chill up Billy's spine.

"Jesus, I hate that!"

HQ =   Lynne family
NYKings = Ralph "the Trucker," and Jimmy "the Rat"
Minors =   Vito "Mad Dog" Vaccaro, Mott Street Boss
                  replacement
Qin Shi Ming-Chinatown Boss replacement
                  Dock Boss
                  ??????????
G-scar =   Griff

Pick up in Australia and Guyana.

"That's in the past, selling the minerals off to who knows who. That may be a matter for Interpol for espionage and war crimes. We need to focus on the connections and fill in that blank spot. That's a key component… getting Griff into our harbor"

"Right in front of our eyes, Billy. Right in front of our eyes. Molly, you could be a detective," Johnny said, complimenting her.

Chapter 27

Johnny and Molly had the elevator all to themselves, an unusual occurrence. Many mornings a neighbor hopped on, going to work, but not this morning. Johnny wore a dark suit, a sober tie loose around his collar. He tightened it when he arrived at the Feed House. He claimed he'd worn enough hats in the Navy, so he went hatless. Molly encouraged him because the brim sometimes poked her in the head when she stole a furtive moment. Besides, she didn't like how it mussed his hair. When he disdained to wear one, he tipped it at a rakish angle.

Molly took advantage of the empty car. She teased Johnny with a sensual glance, licking her lips. She raised herself on her tiptoes, kissing him, adding a little tongue.

"Hmm, nice, Molly. Let's go back upstairs."

"No, hold that thought. Think about me while you're sitting one floor below my office." Glancing at him from under her lashes, she ran her finger up his zipper.

He grabbed her hand.

"Ha, ha," Molly chuckled. "There's that Jewish mother instilled guilt again, even though Oma isn't Jewish. I get it. You owe me—"

His eyes narrowed to slits, Johnny turned and pressed the emergency stop button on the elevator. The car ground to a halt.

"What the hell!"

He backed her into the wall.

"You can't! Someone could see. We have to—"

"Finish what you started," he said, pulling her blouse from her suit skirt.

"Johnny, stop kidding around. You can't—"

"Who's going to stop me?" he said, lifting her skirt. He silenced her with a long, expert kiss, reaching inside her panties to fondle her, then pushing them down. He deepened the kiss, felt her grab his shoulder to steady herself. He unzipped his pants. "Now we'll finish what you started," he sighed, thrusting.

Johnny assessed a dazed and disheveled Molly, a complacent smile curving his lips. He straightened his clothes, took his handkerchief and wiped her lipstick from his mouth. "Time to put yourself together, babe, I'm taking the elevator out of park."

She scooped her panties from the floor and stuffed them in her purse.

When they reached the first floor, Johnny stepped out and held the door. "Tuck your blouse in before you get to the office. Maybe comb your hair?" he grinned.

Molly gave him the stink eye.

"Never start what you can't finish," he admonished. "Only one person will wear the pants in this relationship." *And I don't have the legs for skirts.* "See you in the office." He walked off, whistling. *It just doesn't fly to let a woman take you for granted, no matter how much you love her.*

****

Molly arrived at her office to see Johnny lounging on the corner of her secretary's desk. Louise's face was flushed. She stood close, giving him a provocative smile.

"Am I interrupting?" Molly asked in an icy voice. *A step, maybe two, and Louise would be between his legs.*

Louise rounded her desk with an exaggerated sway and sat. Johnny slid to his feet.

"Just wanted to be sure you are all right, Miss Penett. You're later than you usually arrive. Problem?" Devilish eyes contradicted his choir boy expression.

"Ha! Detective," Molly blushed, continuing to her office.

Johnny winked at Louise. "Sounds like someone got up on the wrong side of the bed. Have to go. Crimes to solve," he said, as he sauntered to the stairs.

****

The day traveled on without the same verve of the morning, business as usual, but not routine. Not one day as an NYC Detective ever is, especially one with the Sabre Blue Society. Johnny pondered the communication from Inspector Laurent, Interpol. Monica, Madame of *The Nostalgia Café*, was dead, discovered in her hotel room in France. Carol Lynne took Monica's journal and Johnny wanted it… desperately. He knew that journal would bring scandal on the heads of more men than just him and Billy. He hoped Monica wrote in code, but maybe not! Possession of the journal proved that Lynne murdered Monica. So, what happened to the rest of Monica's belongings, the ones the Inspector gave to Monica's sister?

Chapter 28

"This is Molly Penett, how may I help you? ... Oh, Johnny, I should've known it was you on the private line. What can't wait until tonight?"

Molly heard his laughter. "I'm thinking of you right now and you're—"

"Stop! Sometimes we put a tap on this line." Molly heard Johnny gulp.

"You never told me that. I guess it's really not that private, is it" Molly's silence gave her away. "Son of—"

"There, there, Detective. Why are you calling me on my private line?" switching to police business.

"Remember when Inspector Laurent found Monica murdered in France? He was going to send us all her belongings. What happened?"

"He gave them to Monica's sister. She claimed her body since she lived right there, remember?"

"Yeah, I guess I do, but now we discovered Monica didn't have a sister. Guess who claimed her body and got all of Monica's belongings? Never mind, I'll tell you. Carol Lynne, the master of disguises and impersonations. That's how she got whatever it is she claims is her insurance policy. You know, the something she hints she'll swap for a deal, if we want whatever it is she has." Johnny knew damn well that Carol Lynne was holding that fucking journal!

"Oh, my God! I'll call Laurent in the morning. It's almost midnight there. What the hell did she do with Monica's body?"

"Ask Laurent."

"I will. Stop on your way home and pick up Chinese, will you please?"

Chapter 29

"Miss Penett's office, this is Louise. How may I help you?"

Shit! I misdialed. I should have called Molly's private number. "It's Detective Vero, Louise. I need to speak with Miss Penett."

"Right away, Detective," she murmured. "H-o-l-d, p-l-e-a-s-e," drawing out her words, purring like a cat. Louise had the hots for Johnny. She didn't care what he and the D.A. had going on. *You never know* was her motto; she held on to that thought.

"Molly, I'm stymied for once." He held his breath, waiting for Molly to burst into laughter.

"Well, Detective, that's open for discussion. Maybe we can talk it over with Mr. Coleman Hawkins later on." Molly heard his indrawn breath, then Johnny's acknowledgment.

"I would love that, Molly, but I'm not stymied over that, you know. Can I talk frankly on this line?" he chuckled.

"What about, Detective?"

"Remember, *they* may record this," his laugh grew stronger. "Billy and I are still concerned what Carol Lynne did with Monica's body, if it was her. Did you get in touch with Inspector Laurent?"

"You must be on radar, Johnny. I hung up with him just moments ago. He is such a nice man, very knowledgeable and helpful. I would like to meet him." *I would love to honeymoon in France and Italy.* Molly obsessed over marrying Johnny and couldn't contain her thoughts as time passed and their relationship continued.

"I'm all ears, Molly."

"No, you're not, Johnny. You keep forgetting part of yours got shot off," smiling.

"Yeah, yeah, I know. We still get a chuckle out of it. You know, Molly, you would like Laurent."

Is he starting to get impatient with the banter? I guess I've got to get down to busines, Molly thought.

"Laurent said he didn't get Monica's belongings. There was nothing at the crime scene except her body. He recalled telling you he would send you whatever things were there after they finished with them, but there was nothing."

"We know that's not true since Carol Lynne has something she's using as a bargaining chip for whatever the hell she wants in return. Anything else, Molly?"

"There's that old quid pro quo. I guess even criminals use it. Laurent said Monica's sister claimed the body after the autopsy. All the evidence he had he put in the report. The investigation wasn't long, maybe two weeks. Monica's sister went to the morgue, paid for her body to be shipped to a crematorium."

"Jesus, Molly. Once again, Lynne played us. Will he send us a copy of their case file? Any indication how she died? Maybe his report will give us an M.O. to tie Lynne to Monica's killing. Cremation puts the kibosh on going back for evidence of any kind. Were you able to get a description of Monica's sister or whoever claimed the body and paid the bill?"

"First things first, Johnny. This is what he sent me in a nutshell. The autopsy just came across the Teletype. Let me read it to you…

Deceased woman found in her bedroom.
Approximately forty-two years of age;
152.4 centimeters tall, weight: 52.16 kilograms.
TOD: one AM

Cause of death: Findings consistent with homicide—Throat cut by a right-handed person from behind. Marks indicated head firmly restrained. A deep, obliquely placed, long incised neck injury on the front side of the neck. The left end of the injury started below the ear at the upper third of the neck and deepened to sever the left carotid artery. The right-sided end of the injury was at the mid-third of the neck with a tail abrasion. There were no other injuries; no hesitation cuts or defensive wounds. No weapon found at the scene. The cut was precise; possibly made by a surgical scalpel."

"There we have it, Molly. All tied in a neat bow. The last sentence clinched Carol Lynne's M.O.--the surgical scalpel. She may have done the same thing to Griff. That could be how he got the scar across his face. How did she get into Monica's room and assault her from behind?"

"Maybe she followed her. As soon as Monica opened her door, Lynne came up behind her. Does it really matter?"

"No, but it clinches that Carol Lynne killed Monica, at least in my mind. It doesn't matter where her ashes are. May she rest in peace. What matters is what Monica had and Carol Lynne took. Maybe the motive for her death."

"It sounds to me, Johnny, like she had some sort of moral compass to take care of Monica's remains."

"Not a chance in hell. I'm going to find out what she did with Monica's ashes. Thanks."

"See you—" The dial tone silenced Molly before she could finish her thought about the Lynne woman slicing Griff. If she scarred him, how is she still alive and doing business with him?

*Dripping water hollows out stone,
not through force but through persistence*

Publius Ovidius

Chapter 30

"Here you are, Detectives. Here is your subpoena duces tecum the D.A. sent over. Saves me a lot of work. Thank her for me, will you please?" requested one of the junior secretaries handing the paper work to Billy.

"I will, thank you," Billy politely answered.

"I don't recognize her. Is she new?" Johnny inquired.

"I've seen her. That was nice of Molly to get this for us. I guess she's just as eager to see who, what and where. Whatta ya think, Johnny?"

"I think she does, particularly if she prosecutes whenever that day arrives."

"You know it will. I guess we have our day cut out for us. Another trip to Yonkers and a visit to Miss. Crenshaw. She reminds me of my fifth-grade teacher. She would stand at the blackboard, a short stout woman with her hair in a bun. I always thought she had little mirrors on the sides of her glasses because she would write our assignments on the board and yell out, 'Bradshaw, put down the pencil until I tell you to pick it up.' How the hell did she know I had the pencil in my hand ready to start the work? I stared at her one day to see if there were little mirrors on the side of her glasses. She yelled at me again. 'William Bradshaw, what are you doing? Go sit down, now.' I found out later when I was assigned to clean the blackboard. I saw them! Two mirrors strategically placed so she could see every one of us."

"And the moral of the story is?"

"Plain as vanilla, Johnny. Smoke and mirrors, just like magicians use. My teacher used the rumor that her glasses had the mirrors on the side as smoke, but used real mirrors to fool us. Carol Lynne and Dr. Paul are using both smoke and mirrors to fool us, like the postmarks on the letters. They must have used that private postal service Molly told you about. What smoke and mirrors are they going to use when Dr. Paul is transferred to another prison?"

"Great analogy, Billy. Let's get up to Yonkers."

****

"Well, Detectives, fancy seeing you here again. I assume you're here for the Lynne Trust papers."

"You are right, Miss. Crenshaw." Johnny handed her the subpoena.

Miss Crenshaw studied the document. "I'll make photocopies, Detectives. You can review them here, just in case you have any questions, or take them with you. I'll be right back." Crenshaw's demeanor was as sterile as a surgical operating room.

"Are you kidding me, Johnny? There's only six pages. I would have thought there would be a book of legal mumbo jumbo that our legal boys would have to decipher."

"Let's take a quick look, Billy. Like she mentioned in case we have any questions. ... Miss Crenshaw left out the bank account. Call her back in here, Billy."

"I'm coming, Detectives. I have what I thought you'd want to see." She carried a ledger she'd brought from the vault.

"Thank you, Miss. Crenshaw. Please explain these entries," Johnny said.

"Certainly. As you see, according to the Trust—Mr. and Mrs. Lynne were such nice simple folks," she gushed, skirting the explanation. "Very cordial. They dressed well. Mr. Lynne always wore his suit and a hat, Mrs. Lynne in her Sunday best. I haven't seen them in some time. I hope they're alright," she paused.

"What would make you think they're not alright, Miss Crenshaw?" Johnny inquired.

"I don't know, Detective. I just have this eerie feeling. Well, as you see," she gathered herself and continued, "Mr. and Mrs. Lynne were very generous to their daughter. They sent her to medical school and all, but she never finished. I never knew what became of that child. I know that each month I wire a sum of money to an account in France."

"Would you tell us the amount and the account information, Miss Crenshaw?" Billy asked.

"Why, yes, it's right here," pointing to the entry of one-thousand dollars a month.

"Jesus Christ! That's a hell of a lot of money," Billy blurted.

Miss Crenshaw made the sign of the cross. Her nostrils flared and she pursed her lips. "You shouldn't use God's name in vain, Detective. I understand you men see a lot of unpleasant things, but…."

"I'm sorry, Miss. Crenshaw. I didn't mean to offend you. We see a lot of horrible things and sometimes words just tumble out."

"I realize that, Detective, but as the Proverb says: a gentle tongue is a tree of life."

"Thank you, Miss. Crenshaw. I have a lot of tree planting to do. We will need all of this information — what, who gets it, and where this money goes each month. How much is in the trust?"

"It's all here, Detective. If you read the Trust document, the monthly amount will differ according to the profits from their investment. The bank is Banque Palatine. That's a patrimonial and investment management bank. They do very well with the funds in the Trust."

"What do you mean, Miss. Crenshaw?" Johnny asked, a bit confused.

"Oh, patrimonial is an inheritance by ancestors like her mother and father. The bank has done very well bringing the total to almost three million dollars. Quite impressive, I'd say, wouldn't you, Detectives?"

"Jesus Christ! I'm sorry, Miss. Crenshaw. That is an obscene amount," Billy muttered. "How did Mr. and Mrs. Lynne earn their money?"

"Well, I don't know for sure, Detective. Something to do with minerals or mining. Something of that nature."

"Thank you, Miss. Crenshaw, you've been helpful. If there is anything else we need, we will be in touch. Billy, if you have nothing else, I'm sure Miss Crenshaw has duties to attend to."

"Good to go, Johnny."

"Very nice meeting you both formally. Remember, Detective—"

"I will Miss. Crenshaw. I have some trees to plant."

Chapter 31

"Good morning, Sunshine," Johnny welcomed Molly's warmth and drew her close to him, trying to give her a kiss.

"Hold that thought. I have morning breath," placing her finger on his lips. Johnny appreciated her beauty as she sat up and stretched her arms over her head before tossing the covers to the side. He gave her first chance at the bathroom for her usual routine, laying back and closing his eyes. Johnny heard her brushing her teeth, gargling, and the toilet flush.

"Your turn, Johnny. If you hurry, we have time before we need to get to work."

Johnny could never say no, particularly with Molly sashaying *au naturel* in front of him. Her beauty was attention-getting, not only to him but to many other men. And she met many men in the male-dominant offices of the NYPD and her position as the D.A. Even so, Molly knew how to stand her ground and ward off the predators that would devour her if the opportunity ever presented itself.

"Thanks for the subpoena, Molly. It came in handy. We got a lot of information from the bank about the Lynne family."

"We have time to discuss business, Johnny. Where's that morning kiss you were about to—"

He didn't need a second reminder.

Chapter 32

Detectives Vero and Bradshaw gave the morning briefing for the SABSO unit. They gave their input for other cases in progress and received feedback on their investigation.

"Johnny, this is a hell of a lot different from daily briefings over at South-Central," Billy said after the meeting. "These are much more involved and on point with great intel for feedback. We impressed everyone with our say in their matters and our suggestions. I guess our reputations preceded us. Their input was good for us too, wouldn't you say?"

"I do. I was especially impressed when it came out that Dr. Paul's transfer could be to NYC... to what's it called... "The Tombs?"

"Yeah, a colloquial name for the official title: The Manhattan House of Detention." Billy dragged out each word in an eerie manner.

"There are four multi-story buildings as high as fifteen stories. I don't know. There's a lot of nooks and crannies even though there is top security—"

The phone prevented Johnny from hearing Billy answer whoever was on the other end. "Holy shit! I guess you made a positive ID or you wouldn't be calling. Can we get a copy of the report? Sure, send it over the Teletype. That would be helpful. Here's the number..."

Johnny stared at his partner, waiting for Billy to say something. He didn't. Rather, he put his head down, continuing to work his crossword puzzle.

"Do you know a ten-letter word for being capsized? The second letter is V," Billy said.

"Okay, Mr. word puzzle. Try overturned, and if you don't put that down you will be overturned in the bathroom where that word puzzle book belongs. Don't bust my chops. Spill the beans. Don't keep me waiting."

"Johnny," Billy said, laughing. "That was the County Medical Examiner's office. They're sending their report over the Teletype."

"Don't let me reach across this desk, and wrap that tie around your neck."

Billy couldn't help but keep Johnny from busting a gut. "All right," he answered. By now Johnny was up on his feet. Billy was about to retrieve the Teletype when he and the junior secretary almost collided, so close to being in each other's arms.

"I guess you are looking for this, Detective." She handed Billy the printed report. "It came across priority."

"Yes, thank you," he responded, tilting his head to get a better look as she turned to leave.

"Jesus, Billy. Really? She's a kid."

"She's no kid. No harm in looking, is there? Here's the M.E.'s report. Maybe you can explain it," Billy snorted.

"Okay, here goes..."

Medical Examiner: 'The two bodies were none other than Lawrence and Mildred Lynne. No approximate age because of decomposition. Identified by dental records. Liquid was Iron Oxide which is a blend of hydroxide minerals plus silica, Titania, and Bauxite. The chemical will break down some to most tissue but takes a relatively long time to turn bone and tissue into liquid. Approximate time of death is twelve to fourteen months.'

"Kinda interesting, don't you think, Johnny? It mentions Bauxite. That's what Griff got busted for stealing. Carol Lynne and Griff might have been in this together. Can you imagine killing your parents, stuffing them into a barrel filled with that shit, and putting them in the garage where you were living? How evil is that? We now have another two homicides to add to our case. We may find ourselves with another eleven murders like Chinatown."

"These two belong to Yonkers PD, although they're thrown into the mix of our investigation. If we ever get these two sons of bitches, we will battle who will get them first to prosecute."

"You know that Molly will get first dibs. She's got a lot of power compared to the Yonkers prosecutor."

"That she does, Billy. That she does. I wonder if our perp, Carol Lynne, did this by herself. Did she have access to these chemicals, as did her parents, or was Griff in on it? And why would she kill her parents when she had all that money?"

"They set the Trust up before they were killed. The date on the Trust is a few years ago. If I remember right, about nine. So, this whole thing gets more involved with these findings—" The ringing telephone stopped Billy from completing his thoughts.

"Detective Vero," he snapped.

"It's Molly. We just got two more bodies."

"Let me guess... Chinatown?"

"You got it. Get this. Shot in broad daylight, fleeing through a crowded street."

"I bet there weren't any witnesses either," he answered with sarcasm.

Molly concurred. "It appears they were running from the opium den where we had those shoot outs."

"Molly, South-Central will continue to have these brouhahas. The situation will never dilute itself. Drugs, prostitution, and all that money. The only way to rid the area of these crimes is somehow make it legal, at least the prostitution."

"It was legal until 1910, when the Federal Mann Act passed; and by 1915, it spread across the entire U.S. making it illegal. I see both sides of it, Johnny."

"I really can't offer anything toward that investigation. It will all come out in the wash, you know that. I will catch up with you later."

****

Hanging up, Johnny knew damn well about the hookers at *The Nostalgia Café*. Monica listed his and Billy's names, along with many city officials, in her journal. Often, he'd thought of the benefits of legalizing prostitution. For one, he and Billy wouldn't have to worry about that fucking journal.

Chapter 33

"Miss Penett, what a pleasure to see you visiting our house now and then," Captain Sullivan said. "Your gal, Louise, called to say you were on your way over. Please sit down. Would you like some coffee?"

"No, no, thank you. I'll just wait."

"I'll get the files and call the Detectives working on the homicides you're asking about.

"Ah, Miss Penett, so nice to see you," Detective Fang greeted her with a genuine gentleman's smile. "Let's see here. We know nothing further on the triple except it was a mob-style execution. All three vics died from one shot, each behind the head. The killer left the gun. That's why we say it was a hit ordered from Mott Street and Vito "Mad Dog" Vaccaro. Usually the gang hits don't leave the gun. They're too cheap. They'd have to buy a fresh one. We feel Qin Shi Ming, our new Chinatown Boss ordered the other two hits. These new fatalities are worse than the others. They mowed 'em down in broad daylight. You already know, although there were hundreds of people around, there were no witnesses. Coming forward would be bad for business and their health."

"So, do you think there's a connection among the five as to why they were killed?" Molly posed her question to Detective Fang.

"Our CI's think the triple was because of a dispute over control of the docks to allow incoming contraband. The double was an example and a lesson—two punks tried to make a name for themselves by robbing the customers and the cash from the opium room. Qin Shi Ming could not allow that to happen. A big number of highly trained armed security have strict orders from Qin Shi Ming: shoot to kill. Obviously, the punks were young and stupid. That incident probably will be swept under the rug unless someone uses the gun to commit another crime and we find it. Time will tell, Miss Penett."

"I want to know about the triple. From your dealing with my office the past eighteen months, the FBI along with Vero and Bradshaw still have two people at large. That pair are still getting opium and women from China into the harbor. We've got to get them this time, Detective."

"Miss Penett we are on this like white on the white rice we enjoy in our culture." We extract intel to a certain point and then it just drops off. This is as frustrating to South-Central as it is for your team. Have you had any success squeezing that crazy Paul guy ... the one who claims to be some type of doctor?"

"Well, no, and he is."

"Is what?"

"He is a doctor, a veterinarian. Between undergraduate work and vet school, they have anywhere from seven to nine years invested. I consider that a doctor."

"No shit! Excuse me, Miss Penett. I didn't mean…"

"No worries, Detective. We've got to get to who's behind the triple. I mean, we know who was behind the hit, we need to know why and who wanted to take control and butt heads with Vito Vaccaro. Can you do that?"

"Miss Penett, we are pushing our CI's harder than ever. They know which side butters their bread. If there's nothing else, I'd like to get back on the street."

"No, Detective, nothing else. Thank you. Be careful."

Chapter 34

"Detectives, excuse me. There's some dame in the waiting area for you both. Says she's an old friend. She insists on waiting, no matter how long it takes. Said she's got all day. She's a looker, dresses nice too. What do you want me to tell her? I could make something' up for you if you'd like," the junior secretary twirled a strand of hair with her finger, waiting for an answer.

Both Johnny and Billy froze for a moment, both thinking of the same woman.

"Can't be Carol Lynne. She'd be insane to show up here of all places." Billy's comment penetrated Johnny's stunned reaction.

"Send her in."

"Johnny, she's not jail bait. Did you hear how she described—"

The door opened, cutting Billy's remark short. Both stood, their first reaction to an unknown outcome. Grace Tilly appeared as if she'd popped out of a covered box with the wave of a magician's magic wand.

"Well, boys, have a seat," she said, sounding like Mae West. "You look like you've seen a ghost."

"In more ways than one, Grace. Sit yourself down."

Johnny wanted Grace to be a ghost, since their on again-off again love making flings had stopped. Grace was a user, and that trait earned her journalism awards and kept her in the style of living she desired. Nominated for a Pulitzer because of her war journalism, she did whatever it took to get a story. Johnny always knew he used Grace just as much as she used him. That was then; this is now. He didn't need or want Grace. He wanted Molly. Seeing Grace made him want Molly even more.

"You know, boys, I may and may not have some information you could use. I'm surprised. You both seem like crabs."

Johnny opened the special drawer, reaching for the bottle of Old Crow whiskey and two glasses—one for Grace and one for Billy. His shot went right into the empty coffee mug.

"Grace?" Billy's inflection questioned her.

"Crabs. They walk sideways." She took a sip. "You're moving sideways, not making any progress on matters I know are important to you. Don't worry, Big Daddy, this time I'm not asking anything in return. This is for old time's sake." Grace took off her gloves, setting them on the desk with her purse, waving her hand to show off something that would catch their eye.

"Grace, is that what I think it is?" Billy stammered in shock.

"Why yes, it is, Detective. I'm engaged to a wonderful man, Clarence Wanamaker. He owns Enchanted Book Publishers over on Fifth. He's a real charmer, like you, Johnny. I hope things are going well for you and Molly. You and Nancy too, Billy. It's too bad I never really got to know you like I got to know Johnny. You look like we could have taught one another a thing or two."

"Well, Grace, so you're engaged… to be married," Billy squirmed to find the right answer. *Johnny, help me out here.*

"Yes, Detective, engaged. It means almost married, right, Johnny? We know all about that, don't we?"

Johnny lifted his coffee mug in a salute, a gesture of good luck. Each tapped the other's glass, joining in the symbolism.

"Grace, you're going back a real long time. You know our relationship over the years has been casual, nothing more. It was mutually beneficial. Now, what may I ask is this bullshit about walking sideways?"

Billy sat there with furrowed eyebrows, trying to follow this conversation. He liked where it was going.

"We all know that two of your prime suspects fled. Knowing you both, you've probably reached a dead end as to what or where to go next. You have Dr. Dean Paul behind bars but you want his fiancé and the other guy too. What's his name? You know," snapping her fingers, searching for the answer. "The smuggler with the big scar across his face. I bet that's not all that's big on him." She leered.

"Griff," Billy filled in.

"Yeah, yeah, that's it. I know that you need to discover who the fuck is getting him into our harbor. It makes great headlines and newsprint. I could write about it in my column all day. I have snitches too, Detectives. That will be your defining moment, wouldn't you say, when you find out who is the actual power for the harbor? I think so."

"So, Grace, what do your snitches tell you?"

"C'mon, Johnny. Does Macy's tell Gimbels? When you get them all tucked away, the headlines will explode. Maybe this one will get me the Pulitzer."

Billy pointed to the framed Daily Globe headlines from the past… cases they solved together.

"Look here, Grace. Those cases will always stand out until you get that Pulitzer. You must remember them. They're all your bylines."

*BUDAPEST HOTEL KILLER FOUND IN FRANCE,
BROUGHT TO JUSTICE BY NEW YORK DETECTIVES;
MAYOR TO BE RE-ELECTED. Speedy trial anticipated. Full
story page six.*

Byline: Grace Tilly

*MYSTERIOUS MEMORIAL DAY BLAST IN NEW YORK
HARBOR.
COAST GUARD CLAIMS UNIDENTIFIED BOAT WITH NO
SURVIVORS!*

Byline: Grace Tilly
More on page 2

"My favorite is about Johnny," pointing, her eyes welled with tears as she whispered her printed words.

*COP SHOT IN CHINATOWN BACK ON THE JOB;
IS OUR CITY SAFE?"*

Johnny and Billy stared at each other; it was Molly's least favorite.

"What I mean," Grace continued, bringing a tissue to her face, "is that you were okay. I have to leave." She picked up her glass and drained it before standing and pausing by the door. "Remember, boys, who really has full control of the harbor. Stop being crabs. The answer must be right in front of you like Einstein's Theory of Relativity, you know? Time does not always flow at the same rate. Do you know how he came up with that? Asking rhetorically, of course. He stared into space from his office window, saw a roofer and imagined him falling. He realized the roofer couldn't distinguish whether he fell under the influence of gravity or just floated in a gravity-free region of space."

"The roofer plummets and feels no change in the rate he falls, only weightlessness, until he hits the ground. Imagine if it were true. Who knows what the fuck would go through his mind as he falls? Anyway, the free fall and the unaccelerated motion he saw as equal. Getting into the harbor undetected is equal to someone who has the power to allow it as one and the same. Like Einstein's theory, it's right in front of you. Stop being crabs. Don't get up, I'll show myself out."

Johnny and Billy stared at each other in bewilderment, pouring another round of whiskey.

Chapter 35

The alarm sounded from the judge's chambers, indicating an incident in the courtroom. Johnny and Billy along with a few SABSO Detectives rushed to answer the call. Pushing their way through the crowd, they yelled, "Stand back! Stand back! Police coming through." Three Bailiffs surrounded a prisoner cuffed to a chair. A doctor scheduled to testify hovered over him, checking the prisoner's vitals. Johnny spotted Molly and an Assistant District Attorney at the prosecutor's table. She tapped her pencil on the pad that held her notes.

"Molly, what happened? Are you both all right?" Johnny's anxiety grew, reading Molly's demeanor.

"This son of a bitch is playing a game of cat and mouse with me and our office. His hearing is a mockery and a waste of taxpayers' money. Every time we have additional evidence, he fakes an attack of some magnitude and it postpones the trial because we have to hospitalize him. It's become a holiday to him. He's cuffed by one hand, leaving the other one free. He gets a comfortable bed, better food, and a different roommate from the prison. He has personal security in the police officer standing outside the door day and night. It's like pouring money down a rat hole!" The tapping of her pencil became more intense. "If it were up to me…" she paused for a breath. "He stabbed his wife and girlfriend one-hundred and nine times and he's claiming self-defense. His Honor has to follow regulations, according to the law."

"Is this the same guy from last year?" Billy questioned, catching Molly's eye. She turned to him with pursed lips and a nod, breaking the pencil in two.

"The Judge will admit him to the psychiatric ward this time, which he wants. He deserves the Hot Seat for what he did to those poor women."

"Old Sparky[4], at Sing Sing Prison?" Billy's surprise at Molly's vehemence seemed surreal.

"That's right, Detective, and I want to be there to view this sick fuck's execution! Unfortunately, there are restrictions against letting me throw the switch! There's no rehabilitating individuals like him. We have all the evidence, plain as day… and then this happens." Molly sorted the files before handing them to her assistant. It was a rare occasion that she herself appeared in the courtroom to prosecute a case. "We just have to wait for His Honor to rap his gavel and announce the postponement until he's further evaluated."

They wheeled the prisoner out on a gurney at the same moment the Judge's gavel echoed in the courtroom with his announcement.

"All rise," ordered the Bailiff as the Judge exited.

"We can go now. How about lunch, Detectives?" She turned to her assistant with instructions for the files.

"Molly, you said something about all the evidence being right in front of everyone. We feel the same way with gaps in our investigation regarding the actual boss that gets Griff into the Harbor," Johnny said. "The ease of Griff's entry is beyond the dock bosses or the three men executed and beyond Vito

---

[4] Old Sparky is the nickname of the electric chair used for executions at Sing Sing Prison
located in Ossining, New York.

"Mad Dog" Vaccaro or Chinatown's new Boss, Qin Shi Ming.
It's like Einstein discovered his Theory of Relativity by
looking out his office window. It was right there, staring him
in the face. Our missing information is right in front of us,
staring us in our faces; we're just not seeing it."

"I didn't know you were interested in science, and of all
things, Einstein's relativity theory. That's a big one for sure.
I'm impressed. Let me make an educated guess. Your science
teacher was a woman?"

"Yeah, I like science. It's like applying certain things to
solving homicides. This plus that equals this type of thing."
Shit! Change the subject.

Chapter 36

Quiet time and Sundays were an agreeable time for Molly and Johnny, not just because of their hectic schedules, but they didn't have to deal with violent crimes or view any horrific scenes. When the arm of the Victrola dropped the needle onto the soulful sounds of Coleman Hawkins, Molly looked forward to an enjoyable day.

"Johnny, you rarely speak of your ex or how you managed raising Angie as a single father. God, you did such a great job."

"Thank you. I'm proud of her and how she stuck with academics before getting serious with a jerk of a guy. Now she's a graduate with a criminal psychology degree."

"I'm proud of you and I'm sure she is too. But there had to be something you did continually to—"

"Yeah, I explained things to her as best I could. If Angie asked me or Simone a question, I gave her the most thorough answer I could without boring her. One time, she asked me why soap made bubbles…"

"Oh, I kind of remember this story, but tell me again."

"I told her there are two different molecules—the soap molecule and the water molecule, just like two different people. The ends of the soap molecules crowd to the surface to avoid the water molecules—they don't want them to stick, you see. Now, let's say you have two people who want to avoid each other and don't want to be friends, just like the molecules want to avoid each other. Who knows? Some of them may be trouble makers. As hard as they try to be friends, they can't be. So, the distance between the water molecules and the soap molecules causes the tension to decrease and friendly bubbles form. It's like when a boy wants to be friends with you and you know he's bad news, you keep him away by having your girl friends around you so he can't get close."

"So, Angie says, laughing at my explanation, 'My girlfriends are the friendly bubbles. I like your explanation better than Mommy's. She said it makes bubbles because it's soap.' I tried to explain so she could apply it in her everyday life. As she got older, I explained every guy's intention with a girl more direct."

"I see how and why you put things in the right perspective and how intense you get on a case," Molly smartly commented.

"Speaking of Angie, since she's working, she's taking over my apartment lease. It's an excellent move for her. The apartment is rent controlled and she can afford it. She can keep all the furniture. I'll get the rest of my stuff and bring it over."

"There's plenty of room, Johnny. I guess we must create something else to argue about so we can have the makeup sex we both like so much." Molly moved closer so she could feel Johnny against her, throwing the covers to the floor. "Your move, Detective. Are you going to arrest me?"

"God, Molly. I love you."

Even accurate information can run awry,
making simple complicated.

Chapter 37

Telephone lines hummed; the pool of secretaries raced the hallways delivering the latest printouts off the Teletype. Intel from SABSO poured in fast and furious like a prizefighter who continued hitting his opponent after he was on the ropes. Were the three men killed because they were trying to muscle their way into the harbor and did Vito "Mad Dog" Vaccaro order their execution? A key found in the pocket of one victim opened a locker at the New York International Airport. It seemed too good to be true, finding so much evidence that led to names, places and some codes. The report detailed the theft of weapons and ammunition from our military and transported to the Cuban Revolutionary Party, helping to quash the growing labor unrest and violence working to overthrow President Carlos Prío Socarrás.

Scrutinizing the data, Johnny questioned how this intel related to Griff and Carol Lynne. *Thrown into the mix, illegal firearms trafficking to a foreign entity, espionage, and spies —*

Billy interrupted his concentration. "Johnny, that was the Bureau of Alcohol, Tobacco and Firearms on the phone. They found some code book they want you to look at. They're sending it toot sweet. I guess your file lists you as a master cryptographer from your Navy days."

"Jesus, the ink on the Teletype isn't even dry yet. The Sabre Blue Society is a machine all its own. I'm hoping this all ties together with Griff and Carol Lynne."

"Excuse me, Lieutenant, this just arrived for you, special messenger," announced one of the junior secretaries.

"My God!" Billy exclaimed. "I just hung up the phone."

"Let's get to work. You were on to something when you said this could lead to espionage." Johnny opened the notebook, concentrating on each page.

****

"Oh, my God! This is one of the easiest ciphers to decode. Even simpler than Caesar's Cipher. I used this with Angie when she was a kid. I gave her what we called our secret letters, just for us."

"Do tell, Johnny. What the hell is Caesar's Cipher, let alone whatever cipher you're talking about."

"It's called A1Z26," he said, laughing out loud.

"A1Z26 sounds like a chemical compound for a mad scientist, although I know you can be a—"

"Billy, listen and learn. I can't believe this," he said, still laughing. "It's so simple, it's almost stupid. I could give this to Angie and she'd de-cipher this. It's just as it's called, A1Z26. The number one equals the letter A. The number two equals the letter B and—"

"All the way to number twenty-six, which is the letter Z. I get it. It looks like a lot. What could be so damning in this notebook that it would take that many pages?" Billy questioned.

"Lieutenant, the District Attorney is on line three for you." A soft voice came across the intercom.

"Johnny, I just got word—"

"Already on it, Molly. We have the book with the codes in it, and we're working to decipher it now. I may be late. There's a lot here."

"How soon do you think you will break the code?"
"Already have."
"I should have known. Call me, please," click.

****

There it was; all spelled out in black and white.

Chapter 38

Johnny and Billy completed the decoding and submitted it to the OIA,[5] confirming intel already in the bag.

"You know, Johnny, maybe we could make our next stop working for the OIA. I kind of like the sound of that."

Johnny just chuckled. "Stranger things have happened to us, haven't they? We need to revisit Dr. Paul. Molly said she spoke with the Governor and he'll hold off his transfer but not for long. Warden Nibley approved an appointment."

"We're gonna have to deal with that maniac being pissed off because his transfer's delayed."

****

The ride to Sing Sing Prison along the Hudson River was like therapy. Their tense, secretive life as detectives changed to a heap of smoldering calm, like the calm Indians experienced after smoking the tribal peace pipes filled with wild weed.

They signed in and surrendered their revolvers and badges to the prison Sergeant at Arms. Billy never asked what they were signing until today–he needed an answer.

"It's a Hold Harmless form. Just in case," replied the Sergeant with a sly grin.

"In case of what? I just sign and never asked," Billy said, his suspicious nature raised.

---

[5] OIA is the Office of International Affairs.

"In case of injury or if they kill you while you are here," he said with a careless nonchalance.

"Can I have my revolver back?" Billy asked.

"No! OPEN!" He shouted to have the gate released for their entry.

Dr. Paul awaited their expected arrival.

"Howdy boys. Give me a smoke, Detective. At least you kept part of your word. I'm out of that laundry sweat box and I am surrounded by intelligent books in the library. I will teach classes soon. It's a start. I'm a patient man, Detective... but how long can a man's patience last?"

"Do you think you can arrange a carnal visit? I would appreciate it, Detective. It's been a real long time."

"Doc, I can work on a lot of things, but I'm not a miracle worker, not yet anyway. Billy, leave him the pack of smokes."

"Thank you, Detective. What is it you want this time, although it's an enjoyable break to the same environment day after day? Maybe next time we can have some pizza and beer. Be sure to bring a carton of smokes next time, you cheap bastards!"

"I'll cut to the chase. Why in God's name did you ever get involved with Carol Lynne to—"

"To commit murder? We had a good thing going, Carol and me. I hate that expression, 'why in God's name'? Does God have a name...one name? I remember a lot of names for God, and I liked none of them. Does God even exist? Why would he allow the bullshit we're burdened with if he or she is such a kind, merciful God? So many murders God allows," smiling and shaking his head.

"Doc, the rant?" Billy quieted him.

"Oh, yeah. Me and Carol. We met by accident. I guess the universe threw us together. Although I worked in the

Medical Examiner's office, I'm a veterinarian. Carol brought her little dog to the animal hospital where I worked before I went to work in the Medical Examiner's office. We couldn't save the dog and had to euthanize it. Carol worked for some shipping company. She said, 'it's just as well because of her travels. She mentioned it was too bad we couldn't do this to humans.' We started dating, and like that," he snapped his fingers, "we were living together in her house in Yonkers."

"Okay, but how and why did you kill people? Her parents were wealthy from their business dealings in chemicals and minerals," Johnny interjected.

"That's right, Detective. However, they were strict and stingy with their money. They felt she should earn her own way in life. They helped her, though."

"How?" Billy jumped in.

"They had ties to a freight shipping company and introduced her to the business. Oh, eventually Carol would have inherited it all, but she was impatient and liked expensive things. I'm sure your women like them too, Detectives. Well, maybe not on your salaries. You can switch sides and join my family. You'd make a hell of a lot more money."

Billy struggled to restrain himself. He wanted to rip Paul's larynx out. Johnny recognized Billy's animosity and stepped in so his partner could get his temper under control.

"Doc, how did her parents wind up in those barrels in the garage?" Johnny tried to dial down the dialogue and get to the facts.

"We put them there. Carol wanted them to die peacefully. We had a wonderful dinner. We did the whole bit—the good silver and china, candles and expensive Cabernet Sauvignon—a real good vintage. Cost us forty bucks a bottle, and we drank several bottles at dinner. Ah! I can still savor the taste."

Johnny and Billy exchanged a look of sticker shock, knowing that forty bucks for one bottle of wine would not tally with their cops' salaries.

"I know your look, Detectives, but Mr. and Mrs. Lynne enjoyed the finer things—clothes, a new car every two years. Carol prepared a delicacy fish dish from the Fulton Fish Market. It was a delicious meal. We laughed, drank bourbon after dinner, told stories. Carol thrilled to see her parents so happy before... before the barrels. We bought opium from the Chinatown opium den and we laced their wine and the booze. They overdosed and fell asleep–all the way to death. I guess 'till death do us part,' gave that phrase real meaning to her parents," he smiled.

"You helped her murder her parents?" Johnny and Billy jolted upright in their chairs.

"Light me up, Detective. Let me try to remember. It was merciful, I guess, with her parents. Both had emphysema from all those chemicals and smoking." He looked at his cigarette with a chuckle. "Who knows? Maybe I'll wind up with it. They were very ill, needed oxygen."

"We never found those tanks," Billy said.

"Carol and I used them to ignite the police car she stole after she killed that lady cop at the airport. We made it look like teenagers torched the car, but we did it."

"So, now you're admitting to multiple murders?" Billy said.

"Detective, don't be so naïve. Many, many, many more. Carol had friends that were bad people. They would do anything for a buck, and she wanted a lot more than what she inherited. So did I. I had a city job and you know what they pay. We were saving all that cash for early retirement. We planned to go live on some exotic island."

"We know about being on the city payroll, but after that we differ. We do honest work and we help people. It's a good feeling," Billy contradicted the doctor.

"Bullshit, Detective. I'm talking real money. I had to work in the Medical Examiner's Department as a cover-up. I got Carol a job so we could use the office to conceal some of our killings when they found bodies and sent them to us for autopsies. It was a brilliant scenario. You can't imagine how much money we were making to kill people. My contract on you two was $25,000. Now, add up what I did as the Janitor."

"Where's all that money now, Doc?" Billy asked.

"Ha! Nice try. Wouldn't you like to know, so you can get it and ride off into retirement? No one would be the wiser. Fuck you, Detective. I have hope of getting out of here one day."

"In your dreams, Doc. You know that'll never happen," Johnny said with certainty.

"Stranger things have happened, Detective. Never say never, just like I won't say you'll never catch Carol. You may and you may not."

"You've got a point, Doc. What can you tell us about the smuggler getting into the harbor and those murders months ago? We wound up with eleven," Johnny asked him straight out

"Some of them I had nothing to do with. You know, the boss that killed himself in prison, Alvise LaPoshio. He had some of them done that weren't mine. I will not confess to any more killings. I'm already in here. Those people killed are… were not nice people. They knew the kind of world they worked in. You know the expression: 'If you live by the sword, you die by the sword.' You both live by the sword. Something for you to think about, don't you agree? Never say never, Detectives." Dr. Paul pursed his lips, eyeing Johnny's mangled ear, a sizeable piece missing from Dr. Paul's attempt to kill him. Johnny subconsciously reached for his ear. Dr. Paul nodded.

"Sounds like a threat, Doc," Billy stated without missing a beat, misinterpreting the thought.

"Call it what you may. A contract is a contract and I'm sure the price went up on you both."

Billy pushed his chair back, scraping along the concrete floor as he stood. Johnny grabbed Billy, stopping him from going for Dr. Paul's throat.

"Let me ask you, Doc. Have you heard anything about guns and ammo being smuggled from here to Cuba for the revolution? Guns that were taken from our military?" Johnny asked point blank, letting the cat out of the bag from the decoded notes.

"Now you're speaking espionage, Detective. That could be construed as treason, and that results in the death penalty! You're both traveling deeper than you might want—diving into a rabbit hole. I love my country. I served it well overseas. We had dogs, horses, mules that needed a vet on the front line. Espionage and stealing from our country? Never!"

"We'll decide what we want to explore," Billy snarled.

"I've had nothing to do with any harbor, opium, or smuggling women for prostitution. You know my expertise. I'm a gun for hire. My suggestion is to set up surveillance, Detectives. You're missing a key component on the docks that helps your boy reach into the harbor." Dr. Paul suggested.

"What about the triple murders last week in Chinatown? What can you tell us about those?" Billy asked.

"I know nothing about them. Do your surveillance," Paul reiterated before yelling, "Guard!"

****

"Johnny, what does your gut tell you? I believe the Doc is telling the truth."

"Truth, Billy? Do you consider what he says or thinks consistent with fact or sensibility? He floats in and out of reality. Yes, he speaks truths on some level and on another one, he would sell out Carol Lynne in a heartbeat if the price was right."

"Maybe we can use that as ammunition to find her. Convince the Doc to give her up and we'll make a sweeter deal, sweeter than the first one."

Chapter 39

"Johnny, this so nice. Just the two of us enjoying dinner, watching the boats, hearing their horns, the salt air. I love the fireplace. You seldom see that in restaurants. It's kind of like a movie setting. Let me say I can't wait for dessert… at home," Molly purred. She slipped off her shoe, running her foot up the inside of his pant leg.

Johnny smiled, blaming it all on the wine. "I love you, Baby. It is nice. You're such a romantic," pouring more wine, clinking their glasses with a silent toast, devouring each other with their eyes. Words weren't necessary. Their gazes spoke for them. This was their special place, a hideaway, one they didn't share with friends. This place belonged to just them—no shop talk, no drama, no dilemmas, no fires to put out. Just the two of them, although something was always present within Molly's hazel eyes—her desire for Johnny's ring on her finger.

Chapter 40

"Lieutenant, the D.A. is on line three for you," stated the voice coming over the intercom.

"Molly, I'm here."

"Johnny, we just got an arrest for the triple Chinatown homicides. It's coming together."

"What's coming together?"

"You told me one of the victims had a key to the locker at New York International Airport where the code book you deciphered was found. The perpetrator wants to cut a deal."

"I'm all ears, Molly." Someone or something always brought Johnny back to that infamous day when the raging bullet tore a piece of his ear off, sparing his life.

"The perp says he got his contract for the kill from someone that works for the government, who got the order from Vito Vaccaro. These three mugs wanted the illegal action flowing into the docks. It looks like they were part of your investigation of the gun running taken from the military."

"Mad Dog," he whispered.

"What? Did you say something, Johnny?"

"Yeah, Mad Dog. What the perp is saying is that Mad Dog gave an order to a government employee, who gave it to this perp who carried out the order. What's the perp's name?"

"He's another Goombah of Ralph Mariozo and Jimmy Enrizzi," Molly threw out for Johnny to absorb.

"Another friend or relative of Ralph "the Trucker" and Jimmy "the Rat." This thing from Italy--what do you call it? The mob has such control, even though these two are resting in Woodlawn Cemetery. It keeps pulsating with new life."

"The Camorra, Johnny. That's what they called it in Naples, Italy, and yes, it will never stop as long as there is money made illegally. We call it job security."

"It tells me your triple homicide ties us together only as to why and who wants control of the docks. There's got to be a shitload of money and payoffs going into a lot of pockets."

"You're talking opium, prostitution, and contraband. You, I mean SABSO, are working on espionage and gun running. It's all part of it. Big money, the docks, ships, smuggling. It's the money that makes the wheels turn."

"We're still working on this gun smuggling, Molly, and the two we're still chasing will tie it all together, even the fight for the docks. We went back to visit Dr. Paul. He denied knowledge of the weapons stolen from the military. We believe him. Although we try to make all this fit, the gun running is separate. We can't fit a square peg into a round hole."

"How is he with his transfer being deterred?" Molly asked.

"He's okay for now. He's in the library and will teach inmates."

"God save us all, Johnny."

"Maybe, maybe not."

*It's always the small pieces once together,
make the big picture complete*

Chapter 41

The decipher code confirmed part of the same information told to Dr. Paul.

Weapons stolen from military for the Cuban Revolutionary Party to help quash the growing labor unrest and violence to overthrow President Carlos Prio Socarrás.

This new twist was live, and being tracked by SABSO. Now it was their chore to put it all together: Griff, Carol Lynne, gunrunning, opium, women for prostitution, the triple homicide, and the identification of the government employee getting and giving orders to control the dock.

"Billy, what are we missing?" Johnny stared in bewilderment.

"Grace said we're like crabs, you know, looking sideways. It must be so obvious that it's right in front of us like the forest but not seeing individual trees and what it's like deep inside. You know, like the question we ponder: does a tree in the forest make a sound when it falls if no one is around to hear it?"

"Sure as shit there's a sound. I'm not hearing anything coming from what we have so far, and it seems neither do you. My feeling is both Griff and Carol Lynne are involved with the stolen weapons. Dealing with selling minerals to the highest bidder, not caring about our country or our position during and after the War tied Griff and Carol's parents together. Maybe you're right. Dr. Paul might like another deal."

"I don't know, Johnny. You'd have to check with Molly and she'll have to run it by the Governor and whoever he has to check with. Who else would we involve in the decision? You know how that goes. It could take who knows how long?"

"We need a plan, a proposal that will seem plausible enough that Dr. Paul will bite."

"You know it doesn't matter. We can tell him anything you want. Whatever we come up with ain't gonna fly. You know it, I know it, Molly knows it, the universe knows it. He's a cold killer and so are his birds."

"What fucking birds?" Johnny asked with a frown.

"Birds of a feather flock together. Dr. Paul, Carol Lynne, Griff and whoever, maybe the government employee who controls the docks."

"Oh, yeah. The perp being held on the triple homicide that's turning state's evidence so he can get a deal. It's a game. Who gets the deal? What's behind the curtain? Choose correctly and you get a wonderful prize."

"Maybe, Johnny, we could get some hookers behind one curtain. Think about what kind of information that would get us."

"I bet you're right. That and a carton of smokes. That would open Pandora's box for sure."

"Ahem!" Billy cleared his throat. "Pun intended there, Johnny?"

Chapter 42

"Johnny, did you pick up your tux from the cleaners?" Molly asked, holding her breath, then taking a sip of her coffee.

"Why is my tux at the cleaners?" Johnny cautiously wondered, standing in front of the mirror with a razor in hand. *What and where are we going that my tux came out of mothballs?*

"Didn't I tell you? I'm taking you on a mystery date." *Maybe this will quench his curiosity.* "You've got a lot on your mind. I can pick it up if you can't."

"I'll get it—"

"Please pick it up by Friday, just to be sure. You'll need it for Saturday."

"Okay, okay." He continued to dress as he grabbed his coffee off the counter. *This must be special for my tux.* "Are we sharing a cab? If so, we've got to hit the pavement."

"I'm right behind you," she said, as they scurried to the elevator.

Stepping in, they greeted the other occupants already in the car with a return of nods and silence.

"Jesus, you'd think people would be more cordial living in the same building," Johnny said as they climbed into the cab.

"They're probably diplomats," Molly responded with a chuckle.

Walking into the Feed House Lobby, Johnny diverted for Willy's Shoe Shine. "Go ahead, Molly, I've got to make a pit stop," thinking there might be some new info awaiting him.

"Good morning."

"Yes, it is a good morning for a shine like the sun shines. Step right up into the chair," suggested the young man standing in place of Willy. "You must be wonderin' where ol' Willy is? You must be the Detective I'm supposed to give a message to. Willy is my grandfather. He told me about you and how I could recognize you. And, I see, it's you all right. My name is Henry. Willy had a heart attack. He'll be good. Just needs some rest and medication. It's gonna be hard for him, and I doubt he'll give up the hooch."

"Oh shit! I'm sorry. Nice to meet you, Henry."

"You want me to hit those Florsheim's, Detective?"

"You're on. What's the message?"

"Ol' Willy said," looking around to be sure no one was near enough to hear. "Look close at those you've been seeing and sharing information with. They're not your friends; some say they're enemies. That's it, Detective, whatever that means to you."

Johnny thought hard and long about the meaning of the message, searching the corners of his mind to make sense of it.

"You're done, Detective. You can step down."

Johnny handed him a sawbuck. "Thanks, Henry. You've done good. Keep it."

"Yes, sir. God bless you."

****

"Johnny, you look like you've seen a ghost," Billy blurted upon seeing Johnny.

"Shoe Shine Willy had a heart attack. His grandson gave me a message from Willy."

"Well, what?"

"'Look close at those you've been seeing and sharing information with. They're not your friends; some say they're enemies.'"

"Incredible how that man can get information. What do you think he's talking about?"

"Fuck if I know. We really have to think about this, Billy. Who are we talking to that won't help us?"

"Let's go down the list. First, who did we meet and speak to about all this? Or better yet, who has knowledge of all of it? We didn't have to speak with them, no?"

"Shit, Billy. That's just what Henry said. Who knows? They're not necessarily who we spoke to. By you saying that, the list just grew."

Chapter 43

"Molly, can you make this bow tie? It's always—"

"I know… more difficult than fingerprinting a perp."

"You remembered."

"Ah! There you go, perfect. You look like a movie star."

"And you look like you belong in Vogue magazine. Maybe we should hop a flight to Hollywood and be movie stars like Bogie and Bacall." [6]

"I don't want to be late, finish your drink."

"Always caring for me, Molly. I love you."

"And I love you." *So where and when is the ring coming?*

****

The taxi pulled up to their destination. Molly could not keep her mystery any longer. There it was in full disclosure.

"Molly, oh my God!" Johnny could not hide his excitement. With all its magnificent splendor and history, he saw what he hoped for one day, and here it was, a gift from the woman he came to love.

"Molly, I…"

"C'mon, Johnny. Let's go in."

---

[6] Film stars Humphrey *Bogart* and Lauren *Bacall* shared an iconic romance including
leading roles together in major Hollywood films.

Johnny stepped from the taxi, holding Molly's hand, taking it all in. Turning, he took her in his arms, passionately kissing her waiting lips. "Thank you. This is the greatest gift. I love you."

"I love you too. Well, let's go," Molly urged.

After spending time in his early career with the Manhattan School of Music, Johnny's dream was to play the cello professionally. Life gets in the way when making plans. But tonight, the only plans were to enjoy the evening at Carnegie Hall with the music of the Philharmonic Symphony Society of New York.

Their seats were first row center stage. Molly pulled a few strings to buy them months in advance at a hefty price. Intermission came quickly, and they headed to the lobby for a drink.

"This is spectacular. I don't know if I could ever match this gift," Johnny whispered into her ear, giving her chills. *You can with a ring.*

"I'm sure you'll think of something."

The lobby filled, glasses toasting, indistinguishable chatter. Everyone tried to get as much in before the lights dimmed, indicating time to return to your seat.

A cracking sound echoed all too familiar to Johnny. The gunshot brought back memories of his pain. He reached for his ear, remembering that day and the blood that drained down his neck onto his shirt and Billy yelling, repeating his name. A murderer made that sound calling out to his victim. This time the sound called someone else's name. Johnny had to keep his senses. He grabbed Molly and pushed their way behind the bar and through a door to an office. "Stay here; don't move. There's a phone. Call it in."

"Johnny, no! Don't go out there, please," Molly yelled, although she knew there was no stopping him. He was a detective, and always on duty, tux or no tux.

Johnny pushed his way through the screaming crowd running toward the exits, hindering his attempt to reach the shooter. He forged ahead shouting, "Move, police, move, police."

There in plain sight on the ground, face up was the all too familiar phenomenon he observed from the Medical Examiner, stemming from the murders in Chinatown last year. The dead man's fall—the automatic crossing of the ankles when the brain dies, and the body hits the floor. Blood gushed from the victim's chest, staining what was once a pristine white tuxedo shirt crimson red. An attractive middle-aged woman stood over him, a gun at her side. She mumbled, "He was going to leave me for his mistress."

"It's okay. Slowly, drop the gun," Johnny ordered. She stood frozen with shark eyes. There was nothing he could do, the man was dead, and she was not. The lobby became deserted and silent. All the gibber jabber from the crowd disappeared.

"I'm Detective Vero." Watching her hand holding the gun, Johnny drew his revolver from his ankle holster. He cautiously approached.

"What's your name," he asked, getting closer. Restraining his movements, he reached for her hand, took the gun. So easy, like distracting a baby from putting something in his mouth. She mumbled over and over; "He was going to leave me for his mistress; he was going to leave me for his mistress."

The police arrived within minutes, bursting through the doors with guns drawn. Molly heard Johnny yell; "New York

City Detective, Johnny Vero," holding up his shield. "She's in shock. She needs an ambulance."

"We've got her, Detective. We'll need a statement."

"Johnny, my God! Are you all right?" Molly ran to him.

"I'm okay, Molly, I'm okay," he said, tugging on his ear. "This was a helluva date. I never would have expected a mystery that solved itself."

"Let's go home and have a drink… a few drinks," Molly said, almost in control of her emotions.

Chapter 44

"Holy shit, Johnny. I heard all about it. Guess who called wanting an exclusive? I wish I woulda been there for the shooting. Not the music, it's not my cuppa tea," Billy stated, eyes lively with excitement.

"Pure murder, right in the lobby of Carnegie Hall. At least we heard the first half of the Philharmonic. It was spectacular. I guess it was Grace Tilly that called?"

"Yeah. Good guess."

"I'll give her a story," Johnny said, dialing her number. "She's been cooperative. Plus, now that she's engaged, maybe she'll keep at arm's length."

"Grace, it's Johnny. Yes, I was there. You want the short version or the long one? I should have guessed it. You always preferred the long version."

Johnny could sense her, smiling. "Here goes, Grace."

****

The moment Johnny hung up with Grace, Billy flapped his mouth. Johnny rolled his eyes and waited until his partner paused to breathe.

"Billy, I want you to make a list of everyone we spoke with or that you think knows about Griff, Carol Lynne, and Dr. Dean Paul. Don't leave anyone out, even if you're on the fence about them. We'll process them out one by one. I'm gonna get us back to Sing Sing."

Chapter 45

Billy remembered Dr. Paul's request to bring pizza and beer. *Fifty percent is better than nothing.*

When they checked in as usual with the Sergeant at Arms, he questioned, "What ya got there, Detective? Smells good. Open the hood, will ya? You know I got to look. Rules are rules."

Billy complied, opening the box. The aroma wafted in the air, so enticing you could almost feel it tickling your nose.

"Hmm… pizza. Looks good too. Did the warden give you permission to bring such contraband in?" He hinted at getting his hands on a slice.

"Why, yes," Billy replied. "He said I could bring you a pizza," and handed him one box.

"You New York City boys sure know how to take care of business. Much obliged, Detective–OPEN!" giving the go ahead for their entry.

"Good thinking, Billy. You gave away our lunch but made us a friend."

****

"Holy shit! You remembered. I could smell it from my cell!" Dr. Paul's avid eyes focused on the box Billy carried.

"Hey, Oscar, do you want a slice of pizza?" he called to the jailer who escorted him.

"Nah! Enjoy, Doc. You never know when you'll get that again."

"For sure, Oscar. Man, this is still warm. So, I guess I have to answer some of your stupid fuckin' questions. What, no beer? Maybe next time you guys can pull some strings. A nice cold beer would go down good right now."

"Doc, one thing at a time," Billy reminded him.

"So, you're telling me I still have hope? How about I hope for a hooker?"

"You can hope. No harm in that," Billy responded, trying to steer the conversation.

Dr. Dean Paul dove into the treat, bite after bite and talking, giving no weight to good manners taught during our childhood: Don't talk with your mouth full.

"Doc. We know you have answers to what we want to ask," Johnny said, hoping he could cut through the bullshit.

"Shoot, I'm listening," Dr. Paul mumbled through each bite.

"We have a list of names. We need you to share what you know about them." Billy thumped the list he'd compiled.

"First, Griff."

"C'mon, Detective. He's a cold killer. If the women he smuggled in gave him grief while they were on board, he dumped them in the drink. He speaks Chinese, so he knows what they jabbered about. You know that Carol's parents and he were in cahoots with the sale of chemicals. Big bucks. Carol must have been and may still be in bed with him. She wanted her parents gone and to take what she felt was hers. I told you that. Lawrence and Mildred had no more to offer. Selling those chemicals was over, and so it was for them. Carol didn't need them any longer. I helped with those. I love her, but she's as bad as him. No moral compass."

"Tell us where she is. Where's her hideout?"

"Ha," Paul chuckled. "There's no hideout. She goes from pillar to post. Remember one of her passports read Lorac Sreknoy. I thought of that one—Carol and Yonkers spelled backwards. She can be a ghost. Here today, gone tomorrow. Who knows? Maybe she's on his yacht. What else do you have?"

"Where can we find these two? That information may get you a nice transfer with teaching a lot of inmates, Doc. They'll never know it came from you," Johnny hoped for a straight answer.

"What I want in exchange for these two, Detective, will really cost you. I mean, really cost you."

"Spell it out, Doc," Billy suggested.

"No pizza or beer. A woman. A conjugal visit. Then I think I can accommodate you. I'll never see Carol again. We love each other, but you know," and he shrugged.

Johnny and Billy looked at each other with raised eyebrows. Neither understood what he meant and didn't care. They just wanted Griff and Carol Lynne.

"That's a tall order, Doc. That is going to take pulling a lot of strings," Billy said, deflecting his request.

"It's on the table. Next," Paul said, staring.

"Mrs. Crenshaw. What's her role?"

"Who? I don't know any Crenshaw."

"She works at the bank that handles your fiancée's money."

"Oh, her. That's it. She's a trustee or administrator or something. The bank invests the money, and they charge fees by how much they make for Carol. She's an innocent old lady that does her job very well. You probably should talk to her about investing some of yours. Any more?" Dr. Paul continued.

"Doc, what about Monica's sister? You remember Monica, the Madame from *The Nostalgia Café*? She was murdered in France. Her sister claimed the body."

Dr. Paul grinned. "Sure as shit. Carol did her for sure. I know for a fact, and she has what she described to me as her insurance policy if she gets caught. It will get her off or reduce her sentence. She found out about Monica's insurance policy. I wish I had one or knew how to get it. I know nothing about Monica's sister or claiming her body."

"Wait! How did you know about Monica and her insurance policy? You were in custody when we found out," Johnny questioned.

"Don't be so fucking naïve, Detective. It's not the prisoner that's the jail bird. The jail bird is how messages get delivered and received."

"Did the birdie tell you about the weapons smuggled to Cuba?"

"Yes, he did. That goes under the category of where to find Griff and Carol." Dr. Paul answered as he ate the last piece of pizza.

"One more, Doc. What about the triple homicide in Chinatown for control of the docks?" Johnny had to squeeze it in before their time was up.

"Ah! Lieutenant, now you're getting close to home. Again, I tell you to put surveillance out on the docks and see who comes up dirty. If I give you that information, they'll find me and do me in."

"Doc, times up," they heard outside the interview room.

"Thanks, Oscar. I'm coming. Remember what's on the table, Detectives." He got up to leave.

****

"What the Doc said ties in with Shoe Shine Willy's message." Billy reminded Johnny as they tried to make sense of Doc Paul's roundabout answers back in the office. "Remember? Who we think are our friends are really our enemies. It's also in tune with Grace's message. Stop walking sideways like a crab, looking in the wrong places. We've got to get that dock under surveillance. How fucking powerful is the Boss that everyone knows what the hell is going on with the docks but won't spill the beans?"

Chapter 46

Johnny met with SABSO's brass to discuss the list of Dr. Paul's requests and his usefulness while Billy set up surveillance on the docks. This would be on the level of confidentiality with the sophisticated unit so nothing would leak, not to dock workers, union reps, or the U.S. Coast Guard. SABSO was familiar with uncommon requests that required manipulation and finagling of the truth. Behind the scenes, they used the SABSO acronym normally used by Sabre Blue Society to indicate their undercover work: **S**callywag **A**nd **B**ull **S**hit **O**ut.

****

"Hello. Vero," answering his phone by rote.

"Today's the day, Johnny."

"Molly?"

"Who did you expect? Don't tell me."

"Today's the day for what?"

"Your pazzo prisoner's transfer to Manhattan.".

"Shit! I know he's crazy, but the Manhattan Detention Center? Its name doesn't fit its purpose. There are four buildings as tall as fifteen stories. Who has the security detail?"

"There's armored transport from Sing Sing with an escort. When they reach the actual location through the secured garage that leads to the drop point, NYPD and the prison police take over. There's a direct route for processing prisoners."

"I don't know, Molly. There's a lot of spaces filled with nooks and crannies for an escape. I wouldn't put anything past his ex-fiancée."

"They're well equipped with sub-machine guns; the high-powered shit you guys love that scares the bejesus out of me."

"Is there an ETA?"

"No! That's all she wrote. Top of the line security and secrecy. You know about that. We have our secrets," Molly snickered.

"Yeah, and happy to have them with you, Molly. You know that. Why don't we plan one of our secrets for tonight?"

"No can do. You're forgetting we have dinner with your daughter. You remember, Angie?"

"Shit! I forgot. I've got to wrangle out of something here that Billy asked me to do with him. His will have to wait. I guess her boyfriend, Freddy, will be there?"

"Yes, and don't be late. He's a fine young man, Johnny. I'm sure you vetted him more than once, knowing you."

"Do I have to bring anything?"

"Why don't you bring Angie some flowers... and some for me."

Chapter 47

Johnny left early to run the errands Molly suggested he do. Although disinclined to such mundane chores to the point of almost an allergic reaction, he complied. He didn't want to disappoint her.

****

"Johnny, these flowers are beautiful, don't you agree, Angie?" Molly asked.

"They are, Molly, and thank you, Dad. That was very thoughtful," turning to Molly with a wink. She knew Molly more or less had given an order. "Dad, Freddy is now a pathologist, and he's thinking about applying at the Medical Examiner's office. What do you think? Can you put in a good word for him?" Angie asked, hoping to help the man who would be her future husband.

"That would be the start of a brilliant career, Freddy." Molly eyed Johnny.

"Interesting, Freddy... you a pathologist and Angie a criminal psychologist. I'm proud of you both. You know that whacko we have incarcerated? His fiancée is still on the lam. He committed a lot of murders with her. They both worked there and used that office to cover up some actual murders they committed. Can you imagine?" Johnny indulged Angie. "I'll see what I can do with the M.E."

"Thank you, Dad. I'm proud of you. I'm happy for you and Molly too. It's like you're made to fit."

The telephone rang. Johnny and Molly turned to each other, questioning who would call on a Friday evening.

"Hello," Molly answered. "I see. That's significant news, Governor."

Angie silently mouthed "the Governor" to Freddy, both waiting eagerly to hear why the Governor called. Molly returned and sat quietly without a word.

Angie burst out, "Molly, the Governor… c'mon tell us!"

Molly smiled. "It's about Dr. Paul, the man your Dad told you worked for the M.E.'s office and committed all those murders. We made a deal with him. In exchange for information, which we can't divulge, he received a transfer from Sing Sing prison to The Tombs here in Manhattan. And Johnny, the Governor told me to tell you that your prisoner is all tucked in for the night in his new cell. All went smoothly."

"I like that. He's living in a new *gated community*," Johnny added for a laugh. "It's more convenient for me to visit with him. Well done, Molly, thank you."

"A toast to a job well done," Freddy said, lifting his wineglass. "Wait, Lieutenant, you visit with him?"

*A smooth sea
never made a skilled sailor*

Chapter 48

The word trickled down to Johnny–the dock surveillance was active. The word came in a sealed folder with a red stamp.

**PRIORITY-TOP SECRET
OPERATION SHORE LINE**

Johnny handed the envelope to Billy. "Go ahead, open it."

Billy slowly pushed it back, "No, you."

Johnny slid it back again. "It's your baby; you set up this whole thing. Be my guest."

Billy slit the seal that kept the priority information neatly under cover. They stared at each other. Billy could have been the TV emcee removing the parchment to announce the winner of the popular Miss America pageant, giving her the opportunity to earn thousands of dollars.

Johnny opened the special drawer that housed his bottle of Old Crow and two glasses, setting them on his desk. "I'm listening," as Billy turned in response to the splash of whiskey in a glass.

"Shall we toast or boast?" Johnny asked, passing the glass to Billy.

"I guess a little of both," he responded, stunned, as he reached for the whiskey. He tipped the glass, downing the first pour. "Hit me again, Johnny."

"Jesus, how many will it take?"

"I'm not sure yet."

The second round went down as easy as the first. "Hit me one more time," bolstering Billy's confidence.

"We can't do this all day, Billy. Hand it to me." Billy slid it over the desk, waiting for Johnny's reaction.

"Jesus Christ! Holy Mother Mary of God!" Johnny spoke the same expression his father had used time and time again. "This must be a mistake; it can't be."

"No mistake, Johnny. No fucking mistake. SABSO don't make mistakes. This will give Grace her Pulitzer."

Johnny poured another round for them both.

Chapter 49

The Teletype printed Vero and Bradshaw's special assignment.

"Good God!" Johnny roared.

"You look like you just saw someone jump off the roof," Billy said.

"Read what the Intern just dropped on us."

"I'll say it this time–Holy Mary Mother of God! We could have brought him to Lilly and her girls."

Johnny thought for a moment, shaking his head. "This is a first for me."

"I'm right with you, brother. Never in all my years," Billy agreed.

****

Armed Detail:
Subject:	Miss Darla Mitchell.
From:	157 East 69th Street
Transport to location:	The Manhattan Detention Center.
Visitation:	Prisoner Dean Paul, Number 33324
Purpose:	Approved conjugal visit.
Date:	Open

"She must be beyond Lilly's class of girls. Note the address where we pick her up."

"This is incredible, Johnny. She lives in the Silk-Stocking District. It fits her purpose, doesn't it?" Billy asked with a chuckle.

"Any word of a big bust for those under surveillance for *Operation Shore Line*?

"Nothing in the updated reports. FBI, SABSO and local uniforms are working together with CGIS to make sure all the I's are dotted and the T's crossed."

"We want to be in on that bust. I want to be face to face with those traitors. They're a disgrace to our country."

"Are you going to tell Molly about our armed detail?" Billy raised his eyebrows at Johnny, contemplating Molly's reaction.

"Can't say yet. How about you with Nancy?"

"Well, she isn't in the know like Molly is. So, no, I won't tell her. No real reason to. She doesn't ask."

"Lucky you, Billy Bradshaw."

"Molly will find out eventually, Johnny. Why not be up front? You know she'll be all kinds of pissed if it comes from someone else. Besides, she has no control over it. It's not her call… even as the D.A."

"Good point, Billy. I need a minute to prepare before I call."

"Want me to give us a pour, Johnny?"

"Why not? Can't hurt."

Chapter 50

Molly wondered what the world and the whole law enforcement system were coming to after Johnny told her of his new armed detail concerning Darla Mitchell. She had no choice but to go along with the scheme, as she labeled it, hoping it would bring forth the information everyone hoped for–the apprehension of Griff and Carol Lynne and long prison terms for both, if not the death penalty.

****

The unmarked squad car drove stealthily onto East 69th Street between Park and Madison Avenues. The narrow tree-lined street with its quaint four-story buildings and beautiful European architecture oozed wealth.

"My God, Johnny. What the hell are we paying for this Darla Mitchell?"

"Here it is. Park and I'll go to the door. Stay in the car. Don't get out, you know, keep your eyes open," Johnny directed, not a suggestion.

He climbed the front steps, irrationally counting them as he went, thinking they symbolized the rise of the light, the sun and a way in to God's path. Ten; he counted ten steps, recalling the biblical meaning of the number ten. Besides the Ten Commandments, ten is the symbol of people's obedience and responsibility towards God's law. Apparently, Johnny reasoned, Darla Mitchell didn't believe in obedience or responsibility toward God, which made him question his own beliefs. The doorbell stared brazenly—go ahead, push its button, daring Johnny to do the dastardly deed. *Why do you think I'm here?* Johnny reached out, falling into the snare of the doorbell's urging.

Darla opened the door facing Johnny. *Whatever it cost; it was worth double.* She was the image of Venus Di Milo, the Greek Goddess of love and beauty, in a tailored gray pin stripe pantsuit.

"I'm Lieutenant Vero," he said, showing her his badge. "My partner and I are your escort. I presume you're Darla Mitchell?"

"I'm impressed… a lieutenant and a handsome one." Johnny postured, not immune to Darla's compliment.

"Yes, I'm Darla. Shall we go, Lieutenant? I've been expecting you," taking Johnny's arm without asking. He escorted her down the steps in silence. Billy jumped from behind the wheel to open the back door for her while Johnny made the introductions. They made small talk, nothing of interest to write home about.

"Lieutenant, do you have something for me?" Darla asked.

Johnny reached for the sealed envelope. He and Billy knew only their instructions, not what it held. "I get that back after our visit," he said.

Billy kept looking in the rearview mirror, catching glimpses of the woman in the city streetlights. She seemed to have stepped out of Vogue Magazine while she examined the contents of the envelope.

****

Billy pulled up to the garage entrance gate where they were met by three heavily armed guards. They checked their vehicle and IDs. Johnny and Billy showed their badges while the third guard approached the rear window and asked Darla for hers. The detectives hadn't considered an ID check and waited in suspense to see what would happen. Would the contents of the sealed envelope get Darla to Dr. Paul? She smiled, adding, "Officer," as she flipped open her ID and U.S. Customs badge.

"United States Customs Agent. Thank you, Agent Mitchell." Johnny and Billy released a quiet sigh of relief.

"You're welcome, Officer. We're on the visitation list."

"Yes, Agent. We ran all of you through the system. You're clear to go."

Billy drove the car farther into the garage and parked. More guards re-examined their credentials, requesting they surrender their weapons before they entered the elevator operated by two armed officers. The guards escorted them to their destination in silence. Once again, they encountered another check point.

"I haven't seen you before. Credentials, please. You too, Ma'am."

"It's U.S. Customs Agent Mitchell, Sergeant, and I haven't been here before."

The Sergeant at Arms didn't conceal his reaction. His expression hardened at the rebuke by a female for his lack of chivalry.

"Yes... *Agent*." He emphasized her title. "OPEN!" He shouted so they could enter the next phase of their assignment.

Darla parted from her escorts and followed a guard to a room for her *interview* with Dr. Dean Paul. Johnny and Billy went to their usual meeting room, awaiting Dr. Paul's arrival, unknowing how long Darla's *interrogation* would take. They played cards to pass the time.

"Jesus, Johnny, it's over an hour. Did you ever—" Darla and Dr. Paul interrupted Billy.

"He's all yours, Detectives. The Doctor got what he needed. He has more information to tell you both. Go ahead, Doctor, spill the beans." Darla encouraged him to repeat what he had told her after their *interview*, which she had secretly recorded in case he changed his story.

"I'm still in never, never land, Detectives. I didn't believe you could get me transferred. And this is the crème de la crème! You kept your word; now I'll keep mine. This is what I know now—no bullshit."

Billy pushed the start button on the tape recorder, stating the date, time and those present, except for Darla Mitchell for obvious reasons.

"Carol Lynne and Griff share a place in Miami. It's perfect for their operation, easy access to the Intracoastal waterway and the ocean. Griff has a great understanding of the waters. Yes, they ran the weapons stolen from the military to Cuba for the revolutionaries to overthrow the President. Cuba is only ninety miles off the coast from where they're staying."

"Who's behind letting Griff and your fiancée get shipments in and out of the harbor?" Johnny went straight to the punch.

"Vito "Mad Dog" Vaccaro. He's been the new Boss for a while."

"We know that," Billy interjected. "He must have someone he gives the orders to who makes it happen without detection." Billy wanted more.

"Sure he does. All I know is that "Mad Dog" has someone from the military on his payroll, but he has control over the entire harbor. I swear, I don't know who that is, but he must be powerful and get paid well. He's also the contact for the stolen weapons."

Johnny and Billy eyed each other, nodding. The Operation Shore Line Report confirmed what Dr. Paul said was accurate. Dr. Paul didn't know the people's names from the military. Johnny and Billy did.

"Doctor, tell them what you told me about Miami," Darla encouraged him, touching his hand.

"No Touching!" ordered the guard from the far corner of the room.

Darla pouted, shrugging her shoulders. "I'm sorry, Officer. It won't happen again."

"Darla said you have information on Griff and Carol. So, what about Miami?" Billy tried to stay calm and not get hot under the collar at pulling each morsel of information from Dr. Paul, making it more difficult than getting a tooth pulled.

"Oh yeah. The address is 18680 S.E. 15th Avenue, Miami. Remember Carol's banker you asked me about, you know that Miss. Crenshaw? She keeps up with the expenses. It's a house on the canal where Griff docks his boat. The canal has ocean access. It's a beautiful place."

"You've been there?"

"Many times, Lieutenant, but without Griff."

Johnny handed him paper and pen to draw a sketch of the interior and outside of the house.

"It must be nice to have all that money," Billy said. He wondered why anyone with all that money would do what she does. *She must be a psychopath.*

"I know what you're thinking, Detective. It's crazy, I know. It's the thrill of getting away with it. She's not well, mentally."

"You told us that Carol killed Monica from the *Nostalgia Café* in France. Did she confide in you what her insurance policy is to keep her out of jail?" Johnny could not stop himself. He had to be sure she had Monica's journal and that it really contained his and Billy's names besides all the prominent officials that used Monica's girls.

"No, Detective. I don't know that one either. She's cunning. There are things she hasn't told me," Dr. Paul assured Johnny. "Believe me, Lieutenant, after today, I guarantee if there is a shred of information I remember or can get from Carol, you will be the first to know. Carol knows where I am and figures you're offering me deals to get her caught for quid pro quo. She's a master of self-preservation."

"We're done for now," Billy announced, shutting off the tape recorder. "We'll be back, Doc. Don't go anywhere," he jabbed.

"I'll be waiting. Bring some smokes. Thank you, and thank you, Darla."

Chapter 51

The behind-the-scenes schemes conducted with CI's harried Molly's conscience, even knowing that it brought forth many arrests. Ignoring her doubts helped to resolve her conflict. She realized if criminals could play the game, so could law enforcement. Should she feel any remorse? No harm, no foul– maybe. It amounted to doing whatever it took to get the bad guys off the street and behind bars.

****

"Johnny, how did the Armed Detail go with your new friend, *The Agent?*" Molly questioned with a hint of sarcasm.

Johnny knew how a loaded question posed by a sarcastic female could lead right into a minefield. *Be careful, Johnny; she's locked and loaded.*

"It went well. I never would have thought–"

"Was she pretty?"

Shit! Here it comes. "Not as pretty as you, Molly. You are beautiful and will always be to me," drawing her into his arms. "You know I love you."

"Do you mean that?" Molly whispered, withdrawing from the dark thoughts that ran amuck in her mind, knowing her man attracted women. She felt his sincerity, became lost in his arms, sinking and yielding. His embrace always left her limp. Her lips screamed for his kiss. He obliged with soft kisses so delicate for such a powerful man. He inhaled her scent, tasting the sweetness of the wine she'd been drinking.

Their kisses grew more intense. Her lips opened, letting her tongue tangle with his. How comfortable, she thought, how well they fit. She knew this wasn't fake. He meant what he said. His touch, his words were comforting to her as they explored each other in silence. She knew she was safe.

Chapter 52

Molly greeted Johnny and Billy, walking into her office.

"Billy, how is Nancy? Please tell her I asked for her."

"Will do," Billy said, getting comfortable.

"We should go out again, the four of us. We had an enjoyable evening," Molly suggested.

"I'll tell her, Molly," Billy politely answered.

"How about coffee? Believe me, ours is better than in your office," Molly joked, calling into the intercom for her Girl Friday, Louise.

"I know you're eager to act on the information Dr. Paul gave to you. This will be the case of the decade. I just wanted to remind you both that Griff and Carol Lynne are psychotic and more dangerous than that serial killer you apprehended in France, Jean-Paul Vincent. My office has cooperated with SABSO and the FBI. You remember Roland Bollinger?"

"From the Chinatown murders," Johnny said.

"He's notified their Miami field office of your arrival. They confirmed the layout of the property from Dr. Paul's sketch. It matches the building department's records. Surveillance is in place on Griff and Carol Lynne. It appears you both will get a commendation--two major international collars. This might buy you both a ticket to the Office of International Affairs. For sure, you'll both be riding in style. I realize now the importance of our CIs. I doubted at first, but now —"

"Isn't it grand when it all comes together?" Billy tried to minimize Molly's doubts. I don't know about you, Johnny, but I'd jump on an offer to join the OIA."

Before he could answer, Molly continued.

"All arrangements are being made for you both as we speak. I know SABSO has its methods of doing what it does best, but all roads eventually lead 'to Rome,' in this case Rome is my office. When you get back, we will get busy on *Operation Shore Line*. We can't do anything until we quash the two in Miami. Without them, there will be no more smuggling of weapons. Then we will concentrate on apprehending the traitors to our country."

"Nothing slips by you, Molly. You're right; all roads lead back to your office," Johnny said with surprise. He had said nothing to her about it. *Operation Shore Line was a Top-Secret document. Some information should stay where it's supposed to stay. But I have to hand it to her; she's on top of her game.*

****

The flight to Miami out of New York International Airport generated the heinous memory of Officer Donna Hathaway's murder. The officer had apprehended Carol Lynne boarding a flight to Italy. Never would Johnny forget walking in to that cell. Hathaway's naked body lay on the cold concrete floor covered in crimson red blood. No one knew how Carol Lynne overpowered Officer Hathaway and where she got the knife. Carol Lynne donned Hathaway's uniform and made her get-a-way in a stolen police car.

"Last call for Flight 808 to Miami. Now boarding at Gate 5," an anonymous voice said in a muffled tone.

"That's us, Billy. Let's hit it."

****

Agents from the Miami FBI office waited at the gate to greet Vero and Bradshaw. They didn't need signs. The Agents had special lapel pins on their suits and had pictures of the arriving detectives.

"Right this way, Detectives. I'm Agent Robert Cook." Greetings exchanged, he continued. "We've started surveillance on those two. They don't know what's about to hit them. I'm glad you could join us."

"We're glad you opted in on our collar, Agent Cook," Billy snapped to clarify things.

"You're right, Detective; my office is running point on this operation. It's just protocol. We decided not to bring in the Miami Police. You know the term used during the War: 'loose lips sink ships.' I'm not saying anything like that would happen, but the fewer in on such a capture, the better." Cook answered, trying to ease the tension and posturing. "They must have a lot of money or someone is feeding the kitty. This place where they're staying is in a very exclusive part of Miami known as Brickell, a quiet, urban neighborhood."

Showing them to an unmarked sedan, they stowed their carry-ons.

"We'll drive by the property. The house is on the Intracoastal Waterway that leads to the Atlantic Ocean, which is the major reason we put early surveillance on them. From your reports, Detectives, these two definitely deserve the death penalty."

"Now I see why your mother loves it here," Billy said as they drove through Coral Gables to Brickell Avenue in Miami. "This is beautiful. Maybe I'll retire here if I can get Nancy to sell her business."

"Miami would welcome you, Detective," said Cook. "We're approaching the house now up on the left. The yellow one with the white shutters—18680 S.E. 15th Avenue, just like your CI informed you. I don't know what it took for him to give up this information, but it was worth whatever it cost your department.

Billy and Johnny exchanged a look.

"We'll do a ride by and go around the block to give you an idea of what we will deal with. Bet you can't detect our surveillance detail."

"When do you plan to hit them?" Johnny asked, knowing Griff and Carol Lynne's ability to disappear. He didn't want to lose them. and muff the operation.

"I expect you're eager to jump on this, but let's get you settled at your hotel. And let me tell you, it's a class joint. Your department must have some fucking budget."

"That they do, Agent Cook. It's a first-class operation."

"Bob, please, as my fellow agents, friends and family call me. We will hit hard tomorrow morning, right after sunrise."

"Okay, Bob, but how do you know they won't bail any time?" Billy asked.

"We have them buttoned up tight. We've got sound and cameras in the house and our agents are on boats next to theirs on the canal, ready to go. That's where we have the monitoring devices set up. I'll pick you up at 0500 hours. Get a good night's rest. Here's my number. I have your room telephone. The hotel has a top-notch steak house next door."

"You're right, Bob. I didn't detect your surveillance," Billy assured Agent Cook, which made him and Johnny less uneasy. "0500 it is."

Chapter 53

Neither Johnny nor Billy could fall into rem sleep, not knowing what lie in wait for them and the agents. Johnny kept thinking of the things Molly said. *'This will be the case of the decade. …. It appears you both will get a commendation--two major international collars. … This might buy you both a ticket to the Office of International Affairs. For sure, you both would be riding in style.'* He reached for his damaged ear, anxious to get home to Molly.

****

0500 came fast. Vero and Bradshaw were at the ready with extra rounds of ammo, field jackets, adrenaline pumping, and a prayer on their lips. Both detectives hoped this mission would succeed even though they did not know how seasoned the FBI Agents were or how they would perform under fire. They hadn't worked together. Agent Cook had many years on the job, and SABSO had briefed him on Griff and Carol Lynne's disappearing acts–second only to Houdini.

Johnny and Billy paced while they waited for the dark sedan at the lobby's entrance.

"Get in; we're ready to roll," Agent Cook directed. He put the pedal to the metal, tearing out of the parking lot while an Agent in the passenger seat operated the radio.

"This is *Rover*. Over to *Sailor*. We're ready to bark. Are you ready for passengers? Over."

"This is *Sailor*. We are ready–Over."

"Twelve minutes to get on board–Over."

"Everyone is ready for new crew–Over."

"Hold position. We're gaining two minutes for guests. Do you copy? Over." Agent Cook tore up the streets with more red lights swirling than a Los Vegas casino neon sign.

"Two minutes and holding–Over."

"Hit it, Sailor," Cook commanded, jamming the brakes to a full stop. They kicked the doors open, leaping from the car. The helicopter whirred above, and FBI boats revved their engines, pulling out to block Griff's forty-footer. Guns drawn, Johnny and Billy ran into the house following the agents, yelling, a police tactic to cause confusion.

"Down on the ground! Down on the ground! Down on the ground! Show your hands… Now!" Johnny saw Griff eyeing the door to make a run for it. Not taking a chance, his fist split Griff's lip, knocking him to the floor. Johnny cocked the hammer on his revolver, placing the barrel to Griff's head.

"Johnny, don't! We've got them. It's not worth your career," Billy exclaimed.

"They'll get the best lawyers. They have the money. The trial will drag on for months. The jury will sit in judgment to determine their guilt. It only takes one holdout with a bleeding heart in that box," pushing the barrel harder against Griff's skull. "Some young lawyer trying to make a name for himself will turn the jury from impartial to sympathetic, convincing them they were insane at the time they committed murder."

"Molly won't let that happen. Her prosecution of cases with a guilty verdict is nearly one hundred percent," Billy reminded Johnny, trying to talk sense into him.

"Listen to your partner, Lieutenant. You don't want this bastard to end your career. He's not worth it. Look around; see how many of us are watching," Agent Cook backed Billy.

Johnny slowly released the cocked hammer. Billy whispered the breath he'd been holding.

****

There they were, Carol Lynne and Griff, spread eagle face down on the floor; their incarceration at hand.

"You think you have me?" Carol Lynne snickered, boldly taunting. "Wait 'til I release what I have. It'll make your heads spin. You, Vero and Bradshaw, will no longer be top cops when I bring you and dozens of the brass in New York City down where they belong."

"Shut the fuck up," Cook commanded her. "Go ahead, Detectives. It's your bust; cuff 'em. Let's get them out of here. Bring them to HQ," he said. "Seize Griff's boat and let's search this house."

"You got it, Bob, replied another Agent."

"We'll stay and help search the place," Billy insisted. "Maybe we'll find something that bears on another case they're involved in. Your office can process all the bullshit paper work before we extradite them to New York."

Johnny nodded his agreement, hoping they'd find the ledger Carol Lynne yelled would be her insurance policy.

"You know, Bob, they won't talk. They're going to hold what they can as bargaining chips," Johnny said, staying for the search.

"Alright. Call me when you're finished," Cook agreed.

Chapter 54

Carol Lynne and Griff, hardened outlaws with no remorse, required added security, furnished with the cooperation of the NYC D.A., SABSO and the FBI. Charter transport out of Miami with six New York FBI field agents accompanied Vero and Bradshaw. Molly arranged for an armored car at the airstrip for their transport. No one wanted an ounce of possibility of escape. They handcuffed the criminals and shackled their legs. First, Molly destined them for Rikers Island, a four-hundred-acre prison populated with over seven thousand prisoners. Instead, she assigned them to The Tombs, The Manhattan Detention Center, the same facility that housed Dr. Paul. Although it consisted of four vast buildings, tight security there minimized their chance of escape compared to Rikers, plain and simple.

The D.A. witnessed the extradition. Molly wanted to see for herself these two criminals listed on the international wanted list.

"Welcome home, Detective. I was on pins and needles and couldn't sleep," she said, brushing against Johnny. Molly reached for him, her hand on his so no one would notice. "Wait 'till word gets out you're home. You're going to be one active guy with all this, and believe me, you'll be busy with me over the next few days."

Johnny listened with his good ear while he watched the prisoners.

"Don't forget the press will kick down your office door and shadow you no matter where you go. I'm sure Grace

Tilly is chafing at the bit to get an exclusive from you, Big Boy!" She looked up at him with shining eyes. "I'm proud of you. I spoke to Angie to let her know you're back. She's very relieved."

"I'm glad I'm home too, Molly, with you," Johnny whispered.

"This was one hell of a perilous mission. You and Billy will have to meet with the Mayor and Governor shortly."

"They're ready to move them out of the truck. I have to go," he said, drawing his revolver.

"I love you," Molly mouthed, letting go of his hand.

Chapter 55

Molly rolled out of bed and made a beeline for the shower. Johnny enjoyed looking at her nakedness. Her curves and valleys set him on fire. He couldn't imagine her not being in a relationship all these years. At least they hadn't discussed it.

One thing for sure, Molly was glad Johnny divorced Simone years ago, and she was now his.

****

"Johnny, Dr. Paul will be distraught when he learns his fiancée is in the women's building next to his and he can't touch her. Or is she his ex-fiancé?" Molly frowned, then her brow smoothed. "So close, and yet so far away. What kind of deal do you suppose either would make if they could be together regularly?" Molly speculated aloud.

"Don't forget; he gave her and Griff up. She would doubtless scheme to kill him for this. He kept his word after, you know…"

"Do I? That arrangement will go down in our history books for sure. But mixing actualities can make for strange bedfellows." The thought shook her complacency. *Grace Tilly had used Johnny as an IOU for getting him the information from her newspaper to see who placed those ads for Dr. Paul to kill people.* Molly made certain he and Grace would never become strange bedfellows ever again.

"Molly, are you alright?" Johnny broke Molly's silence.

"Yeah, I'm good. Now that we have the Three Musketeers secured, it's time for *Operation Shoreline*. Our offices worked extensively while you and Billy were risking your lives bringing Griff and Carol Lynne to justice. The entire world should know what you—" Molly teared up, unable to continue.

"I love you, Molly." Johnny pulled her into his warm embrace.

"I love you too. I'll be okay." Her face softened. "We have a meeting today in Agent Bollinger's office with SABSO and the military. Now I have to fix my makeup."

****

"All present and accounted for," FBI Agent Bollinger said aloud, checking his roster. "Let's begin. Hit the lights." The room darkened except for the light from the presentation screen. "Look at the surveillance from our counterpart, Captain Hennessey. He's the officer in charge of *Operation Shoreline*."

"We've seen our suspects here," he pointed, "at the docks at varying times, both together and separately. Look closely at the next slide. Here's our number one suspect meeting with none other than the new Mob Boss, Vito "Mad Dog" Vaccaro's right-hand man. Vaccaro never meets with anyone in the open. He sends his henchmen. Now we know who got paid to let Griff and Carol Lynne drop the women and drugs and load the weapons. Since their arrest, we assume our suspects will have to find someone else because Mr. Vaccaro has our suspects tied to his hip."

"This next slide shows dock hands unloading dark green crates marked U.S. Military Ordnance. They stamp star roundels on them to distinguish their destination–Cuba. They steal them from our Fort Hamilton Watervliet Arsenal here in New York City," Agent Bollinger concluded.

Molly leaned into Johnny, whispering, "The Governor is going for the death penalty for Griff and Carol Lynne. Griff is transferring to Sing Sing Prison and Carol Lynne to West Field State Prison for women, both maximum security prisons. The transfers will be soon. Hopefully, by the time word hits Dr. Paul, she'll be away."

"Ahem," Hennessy cleared his throat, getting Molly's attention. "We move in the morning at 0700. We'll convene at Pier 79 and bring these traitors into our custody for court martial. I am proposing life in prison," announced Captain Hennessey. "If there are no questions," he paused. "Meeting dismissed."

Chapter 56

Molly could not accompany the task force. She was confident Johnny could take care of himself, but she still worried. Every takedown was dangerous. Yet, she knew when she entered a relationship with him that his job entailed danger, hardened criminals, weapons, and maybe, just maybe.... The gnawing in her gut kept her awake most of the night. She finally dozed and woke to the sound of the shower. She paused for a moment, concealing her fears before reaching out to read the clock—4:30 AM. Maybe she'd gotten three uninterrupted hours of sleep, getting up to join Johnny in the shower.

"I tried not to wake you. You had a rough night."

"Never think about sneaking away. I never want you to leave on an assignment without waking me... Never! Am I clear?"

"Yes, Madam District Attorney... as crystal." He pulled her closer, letting the water cascade over them as soap suds ran off their bodies and swirled down the drain.

****

Johnny and Billy arrived right on the dot, greeting everyone involved in the takedown. Hennessey had an Army truck waiting to transport them, and even dozen and all heavily armed. This was a life and death situation, and no one wanted any slipups. What the two men listed on the arrest warrant would have in mind when confronted was anyone's guess. They faced a military court-martial, charges of arms trafficking, and treason in the sale of weaponry to an enemy nation. The resulting disgrace in view of the entire nation would shame them and humiliate their families. Government officials and the military will want their heads on a platter and push for the death penalty. Best case scenario, they faced a life sentence at Leavenworth Prison.

The task force rode in a tense silence, each occupied with his own thoughts, hoping their assignment would get done without a hitch, and every man would return home safely. The sun had not risen; the early morning breeze off the water was chilling. The truck's tent-like canvas cover helped, but not much.

The truck halted at the guard gate, signaling their entry. All aboard hit the ground. The sound of their feet pounding on the wooden slats of the dock gave off an ominous cadence, like the gallop of wild horses coming closer and closer. The helicopter hovered above, lighting up the area leading to the Commander's office.

"Darby, what the fuck is going on? What is that? Get up," shouted Commander Cunningham.

"Oh, no! No, no, no," Bosun Darby shrilled. "I never thought this day would come."

The door burst open. Twelve armed men pointed their weapons at Fred Cunningham and Bosun Darby.

"Commander Cunningham and Bosun Darby, you are under arrest," ordered Captain Hennessey, in a cold, no-nonsense voice. "I'm sure you know why."

"Jesus Christ, Fred, you had to know this day would come. How could you betray your country, your uniform, your family?" Johnny added with disgust.

Cunningham grabbed Darby using him for a shield. He drew Darby's sidearm from his holster, pointing it to Darby's head.

"Commander, what are you doing? They've got us, can't you see?" Darby said, trembling.

"Shut the fuck up, Darby," Cunningham barked.

"Fred, what are you doing? Don't be stupid. Put the gun—"

BLAM! One shot to Darby's head. He slumped, falling to the floor.

BLAM! Cunningham used another shot on himself.

"Jesus Christ, I didn't see that coming," Johnny said, shaking his head and looking down at the splatter of blood and brain matter reminiscent of an avant-garde painter's canvas displaying a new work of art.

"Well, that just moved us back a few squares. The information they had would have been invaluable," Billy mumbled.

"We've stopped a lot of crime and the last one will get you detectives some commendations for halting gun running of U.S. Military weapons to Cuba. Cunningham took the easy route for the both of them, although not so for their families," Hennessey said, making the sign of the cross. "May God have mercy on their black souls."

"I hope not." Turning to Johnny, Billy whispered, "We still need to find that fucking journal. I don't want to wind up on the floor like these two."

Thank you for choosing my novels.
Having you as a reader is an important part of my journey
as an author.

Your opinion matters to me.
One way to enrich readership is with reviews.
Amazon, Barnes & Noble, Kindle, and Nook,
as all online booksellers, use reviews
in their algorithms for book placement.

Please place a review on Amazon.com for me.

Thank you again. I hope you'll look for my next novel.

fred berri

About the Author

Mr. Berri graduated from Columbia State University with an online business degree. He relocated his family to Florida from New York, spending years as a Financial Specialist with one of the largest banking institutions in the U.S. He has volunteered teaching Junior Achievement in the Florida public school district. In addition, he led a volunteer group for a reading program for grades K-3. Throughout his career, he has done public speaking and appeared in several TV commercials, including voice-overs. Berri has written numerous murder mysteries and children's books, which are listed on his website: fredberri.com.

References

CI: Citizen informant.

Hoosgow: jail.

Dick: A popular term for cops originated from the Dick Tracy
cartoons of which the title character is a Detective.

Bosun: Ship's officer in charge of equipment and the crew.

G P: General Population.

Last Rites: A ceremony meant to prepare the dying person's soul
for death, by providing absolution for sins by Penance.

Delmonico's Steak House, N.Y.C: Delmonico's is the name of
various New York City restaurants of varying duration,
quality, and fame. The original and most famous iteration
was operated by the Delmonico family at 2 South William
Street in Lower Manhattan during the 19th and early 20th
centuries, when it gained a reputation as one of the nation's
top fine dining establishments.

The No It Awl Jazz Club: A fictitious night club created by
author, fred berri. The name has been used in the other series
featuring Homicide Detective Johnny Vero.

Jumpin' Jehoshaphat: On consulting the Oxford English
Dictionary and the Random House Historical Dictionary of
American Slang, it seems clear that the name of the king of
Judah, most commonly Jehoshaphat, was used in the United

States around the middle of the nineteenth century as a
euphemism for Jesus. The phrase Jumping Jehoshaphat is first
recorded from Mayne Reid's Headless Horseman of 1866.

Dick Tracy and Catchem: Dick Tracy is an American comic strip
(originally Plainclothes Tracy), a tough and intelligent police
detective created by Chester Gould. It made its debut on
Sunday, October 4, 1931, in the Detroit Mirror.

Sam Catchem: A pun on "catch them," being Dick Tracy's
Detective partner.

Irish Sweepstakes: The Irish Hospital's Sweepstake was one of
the largest lotteries promoted internationally, authorized by
the Irish government to benefit Irish hospitals. It was never
legal in the U.S.

Variety: An American media company founded by Sime
Silverman in New York in 1905 as a weekly newspaper
reporting entertainment news and reviews on theater, shows
and vaudeville.

Coleman Hawkins: An American jazz tenor saxophonist- 1904-
1969. Molly's favorite jazz tenor saxophonist, a/k/a 'Hawk.'

Your Hit Parade: Your Hit Parade was an American radio and
TV music program broadcast from 1935-1953 on radio.

Shit from Shinola: A colloquial expression used to designate not
knowing the difference between Shinola, a shoe polish, in this
case brown, which partly explains the derivation without
putting too fine a point on it.

196 | fred berri

Subpoena duces tecum: A writ commanding a person to produce
in court certain designated documents or evidence.

Philadelphia Lawyer: A term to describe a lawyer who knows
the most detailed and minute points of law.

Enchanted Book Publishers: A fictitious book publisher by
author, fred berri.

Macy's & Gimbels: Two of the largest national department stores
that rivaled each other.

Rent Control: Rent control is a government regulation limiting
the price a property owner can charge a tenant to live in a
specific apartment.

ATF: Bureau of (Alcohol-Tobacco-Firearms, an agency of the U.S. Department of Justice that protects our communities from violent criminals, criminal organizations, the illegal use and trafficking of firearms, the illegal use and storage of explosives, acts of arson and bombings, acts of terrorism, and the illegal diversion of alcohol and tobacco products.

Miss America: A beauty pageant that has been around since 1921. It started out as a bathing suit contest designed to attract tourists to Atlantic City, New Jersey. In the almost one hundred years since, it has grown into a huge organization that provides scholarships to women and encourages female empowerment.

CGIS: The Coast Guard Investigative Service (CGIS) is a division of the United States Coast Guard that investigates crimes where the U.S. Coast Guard has an interest. Established in 1915.

Acknowledgments

Formatting by Janet Sierzant – La Maison Publishing, Inc.
Editor - Judith Konitzer.

Cover: NYC Detective Badge and Internal Picture of Sabre:
Google photo stock images.